A GRASS ROPE

Other books by William Mayne

THE GLASS BALL
UNDERGROUND ALLEY
THE BLUE BOAT

WILLIAM MAYNE

A GRASS ROPE

Illustrated by Lynton Lamb

NEW YORK

E. P. DUTTON & CO., INC.

TO
HIS GRACE
AND MRS FISHER

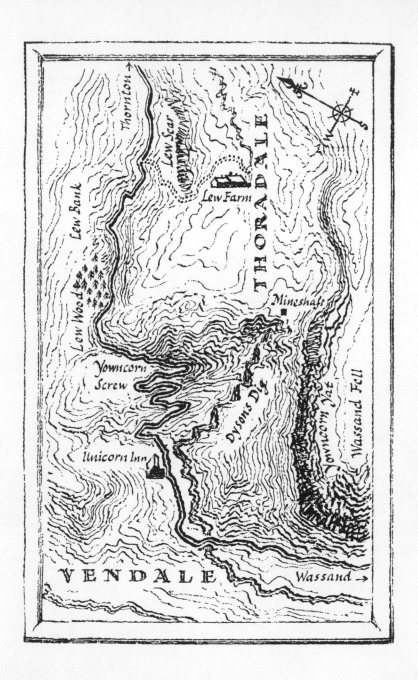

CONTENTS

CHAPTER ONE

HOUSE PAINT

Nan passed eggs out one by one to Mary, who put them in the basket. One hen was sitting lazily in a nesting box in the warm sunlight. Nan pulled her out and sent her off in a cloud of chaff and feather dust and warm hen smell and squawk.

'Brown eggs,' said Nan. 'Shall I write you one, Mary?'

'Of course you must,' said Mary. 'Have you got a pencil?'

Nan always brought a pencil when she collected eggs, in case there were some brown ones that must be written. She wrote her own name on one egg: Nan Owland, and on the second Mary Owland. Mary put them in the basket with the rest: they would be sorted out when the eggs were washed.

Nan carried the eggs across the field. Mary rode her tricycle, steering round the dust pits the hens had scratched themselves; and round hens that would take no notice of her.

Charley came up the valley from his home, riding his bicycle along the sheeptrack beside Thora Beck, across the plank bridge over Lew Gill, and into the farmyard. He was Daddy's farmhand, and he had just had his breakfast.

'How do?' he said. 'Grand morning.'

'A lot of eggs, too,' said Mary.

'Aye,' said Charley. 'The hens is starting to like t' sunshine.' He leaned his bicycle against the wall beside the tractor. He reached up and brought from its hooks the tray that fitted behind the tractor: the milk churn had to go up to the Bank ready for collection.

Mary's tricycle had a tray in the same place: behind the seat and between the wheels. She took some of the eggs and carried them to the kitchen in it. Charley started the tractor, put the axe and the full milk can in the tray, and drove out round the house.

Mary unloaded the eggs, raced out of the kitchen, passed the tractor, and opened the gate for Charley. Then she travelled up to the road in the tray of the tractor, sitting between the milk churn and her red tricycle. She sat on the handle of Charley's axe, and that helped to stop her from sliding down into the back of the tray. Charley put one hand down behind him and held the belt of her coat.

He had to let go on the steep sharp corner on Lew Scar, where the rock stuck out of the hill in a step five fields across. Mary knew the corner, and held on to the sides of the tray; but the axe slid under her, and the tricycle folded its front wheel and waved its handlebars, and spun its pedals. But they all stayed in the tray. Charley's hand came down and caught her belt again.

'Tha 'rt ower early to go off to school,' he said.

'I shan't go to school before my breakfast,' said Mary. 'Nor on Saturdays.'

The tractor was at the top of the lane now. Charley stopped at the gate.

'Wilt oppen it?' he asked Mary. Mary was already out of the tray and lifting the tricycle out after her. She rode round the tractor and opened the gate. Charley drove through, to the stand where the milk churn had to go.

'Shut t' yat,' he said. 'Ah'm to go up to Lew Wood for a tree.'

'I'll come with you,' said Mary. 'I'll leave my tricycle behind the gate.'

'Bring it wi' thee,' said Charley. 'Or happen tha mun walk back down.' He swung the full churn up on to the stand, and sat on the seat of the tractor again.

'Can I ride behind and hold on?' asked Mary. 'I won't fall off.'

Charley was looking down the Bank, not at her. He was saying 'How do?' to somebody walking and wheeling a bicycle up Lew Bank from Thoradale.

'Ah'll give thee a pull to t' top,' he said. 'Put thy can in t' tray.'

'Well, thanks,' said the walking cyclist. 'It's a bit of a way from Thornton up here.'

'It is that,' said Charley. 'Put yon tricycle and t' bairn in t' tray as well.'

The cyclist lifted the tricycle in, and Mary climbed in alone.

'Set?' asked Charley. The cyclist laid his left arm along the mudguard; Charley put the tractor in gear; they swung in a half circle and began to climb the bank.

Mary looked down into the valley to watch the farm come into sight. It was still hidden: all she saw was the

jaggy top of Lew Scar and the grey rock of the far side of the valley, sparkling in the sun with newly grown green: all varnished with dew.

She saw smoke from the kitchen chimney. The smoke hung in the air like wool in a wire fence.

The tractor climbed up and up. They passed the western buttress of Lew Scar, and the farm seemed to move along with them and into sight. Mary saw Nan in the yard, with a basket in her hand. Mary waved, but Nan did not look up.

The road turned a little towards the south. Mary saw the ends of the farm building; then the sunlight began to pour from the crest of Wassand Fell into her eyes, and she could no longer look down the dale.

She first looked down at the can in the corner of the tray. It was marked 'House Paint' and the colour was green. There were no houses you could paint in Lew Bank, or on Lew Fell. Perhaps it was only to paint a gate. But no one would cycle from Thornton to paint a gate on Lew Fell.

Mary looked at the cyclist. He was still resting one arm on the mudguard and steering the bicycle with the other. The tractor was going slowly up the slope, and the bicycle had too little way on it to balance alone; the cyclist had to pull himself in to stay with the tractor at all, and push himself out to stop himself from falling against the black mountaineering tyre of the big wheel.

Mary at first thought he was a man; but he was wearing a Thornton Grammar School cap, with the same colours and shield as Nan's; but with a red circle at the top: so he must be only a boy. Perhaps he was going to paint his bicycle. Even then Lew Bank was a queer place to come to.

They came to the unexpected top of the Bank. Instead of leaning backwards the tractor leaned forwards. Mary slid back and banged her head on the seat. The tricycle and the can of paint slid with her. Charley put the brake on and stopped the tractor from moving. The cyclist let go and put his foot on the ground.

'This is t' top,' said Charley.

'Thank you,' said the cyclist. 'It's pretty steep up Thoradale, isn't it?'

'Aye,' said Charley. 'You're out o' Thoradale now. This side is Vendale. Are you off down theer?'

'Yes,' said the cyclist. 'Unicorn Inn.'

'It's downhill,' said Charley. 'But tha 'd best walk. Lew Bank is nowt. T'other side, into Vendale, is wicked. Yowncorn Screw, they call it, after Yowncorn Yat yonder. Very nigh as steep, too.'

Yowncorn Yat was a great black cliff on the edge of Wassand Fell. The shoulder of the fell came humping up from Thoradale and looked over Vendale and the pass into Thoradale. And then, at the highest hump, the shoulder was chopped away to the flat cliff two hundred feet high, and a quarter of a mile across. The sun was at the back of it now; the fell itself was soft with mist from the heather, and the dry cliff stood black, as if the night still lingered there. Yowncorn Yat could be seen from Thoradale and Vendale for miles either way.

'It's called a yat,' said Charley, 'but there's no road theer. It's a yat for getting in, Ah 've heerd: getting into t' Fell.'

A yat is a gate, but Charley thought 'gate' was a new-fangled word and always said 'yat'.

'Way in?' said the cyclist. 'What for? Who goes into the Fell?'

'Summat,' said Charley. He would say no more, because Mary was there to hear. But Mary knew about Yowncorn Yat.

'The hounds went in,' she said. 'They go hunting all the way under the fells. You hear them, and it's bad luck.'

'Tha 's niver heerd nowt o' t' soart,' said Charley.

'People have heard them,' said Mary.

'Best not to,' said Charley. 'Anyroad, it's nobbut a tale. But do thou walk down t' Screw, lad, not ride.'

6

'Thank you,' said the cyclist, 'I will.'

Mary picked up the can of paint. The cyclist took it under his arm and rode off carefully; the slope was still only mild, though it would later become sharp.

'Now,' said Charley, 'take out thy grid.' Mary took out the tricycle, and stood it in the rough grass by the wall. Charley turned the tractor round and stopped the engine. Mary took the axe from the tray, and they went over the wall into Lew Wood.

'It's them little foxes after thy dad's fowls,' said Charley. 'Nest o' them under t' Yat. They've been ower yon side mostly; but happen they'll be back. We mun get summat for fence posts.'

He chose a small tree, took the axe from Mary, and brought the sapling down with ten blows. The chipped wood was white, veined with red. The chips were sticky, and smelt like snow. Mary warmed a piece in her hand, and smelt it again; but the scent had changed to dry moss.

Charley ripped off the branches of the fallen tree, and sliced the trunk in three pieces. It bounced and leapt under the blows. The axe sounded dull if you listened only to the echo from the other trees. If you listened to the stroke itself you heard the blade gnaw and fracture the wood fibres.

'Theer, that'll do,' said Charley. Mary took the axe and put the hot sticky blade against her cheek. The steel smelt like a knife that has cut an apple.

Charley gathered the three pieces of trunk under his arms, and carried them to the wall. Mary brought one fronded twig with pale needles amongst the old green.

Charley threw the wood over the wall and climbed after it. His toes left white scratches on the grit wall, and his iron heels sparked when they kicked the top stones.

The wood and the axe filled the tray of the tractor. Charley lashed a couple of yards of cord across the top to hold the load in place. He gave Mary another piece. She knew what to do with it. One end she tied to the front axle of the tractor; the other she tied to the back of the tricycle. Charley started the tractor.

'Set?' he asked.

Mary waved, and began to pedal. Charley let the tractor follow slowly. The cord pulled tight. Mary pulled the tractor, and the tractor held her back on the slope.

They arrived at the farm with Mary out of breath from pulling downhill so hard; the tractor stood with its engine chuckling slowly. Mary loosed the cord from the axle and rode round the house.

Nan was in the yard, washing the morning's eggs.

'I want to do some of those,' said Mary.

'You haven't washed yourself even,' said Nan. Mary's face had a dark line where tree dust from the axe had stuck to it.

'We've been bringing wood,' said Mary. 'Charley and I. A whole tree. And we pulled a man up the Bank on his bicycle. At least he wasn't a man, he was a boy from the Grammar School. Do you know him?'

'I expect so,' said Nan. 'What did he look like?'

Mary was no good at explaining. 'He had a red ring round the top of his cap.'

'A prefect,' said Nan. 'He'd be quite old. I mightn't know his name. I've never spoken to any of the prefects.'

'But you've been there a long time,' said Mary.

'Two terms,' said Nan. 'But I've never done anything wrong. At least, not when a prefect's been there.'

Mary helped to wash the eggs, and counted them, and stacked them in the trays putting aside the named brown ones. She entered the number in the book, and put it back on its nail. Then she trod on Dump the house dog, tripped over the cord still trailing behind the tricycle, and emptied the egg-washing water over her feet. She threw the cloth at Nan for laughing, and they both went into the kitchen because breakfast was ready.

'You'll have to wash it after breakfast,' said Mother, looking at Mary's face. But Mary had to do it almost at once: she was so thirsty after pulling the tractor that she drank until she began to swallow tea-leaves, and spluttered them back all at once. She was sent out to wash them off and count a hundred. She was not away long, because she jumped from seventy-nine to ninety without knowing. When she came back Daddy was talking about the little foxes.

'They'll go away in a month or two,' he said. 'But just now they're all together, and very hungry; and even if they weren't very hungry, when they get among fluttering birds they snap the heads off any in sight.'

'They're pretty animals,' said Nan.

'Most animals are,' said Daddy. 'But these are too fond of feathers. They must stuff pillows with them.'

'I'd like to live with some furry foxes on pillows,' said Mary. 'In a hole. They could have collars and pull me on my tricycle.'

'You wouldn't like to live against Yowncorn Yat,' said Nan. 'Not with the hounds inside.'

'Never mind about stories,' said Mother. 'Eat your porridge, Mary.'

'Queen of the foxes,' said Nan. 'Where would you live?'

'Not near Yowncorn,' said Mary. 'Vendale is an empty world, and I'll live there.'

CHAPTER TWO

SOMETHING GREEN

There was a new roll of wire netting, six feet tall, firm and springy and white. Daddy brought it down from the rafters of the tractor shed. He had to brush off a cobweb from his head, and remove gently a spider that was acting as a left ear ring.

'It's like a wig factory up there,' he said.

Nan let the netting lean against her shoulder blades until Mary brought the tricycle. Nan lowered the top end to saddle level and held it whilst Mary lashed her tractor-dragging cord round it.

'You've hanked a pigtail in,' said Nan. Mary disbelieved her, and stood up to get on to the saddle: she left behind a ribbon and a snarled up twining of hair: blue ribbon and yellow hair in the silver-white meshes.

'She'll need the wig,' said Daddy. Mary began to pedal away. Nan caught the other end of the roll as it went past and held it off the ground. Daddy brought a mattock, a hammer, and a pocketful of staples.

The three posts were lying on the ground where Charley had left them on his way up to the fellside.

'It takes the dickens of a time to dig posts in this field,' said Daddy. 'Last time I did it I began to think it would be quicker to build a wall with the stones I unearthed. And after I've done it all, I don't suppose the foxes will have dreamed of coming near.'

'Watching from the Yat and laughing,' said Nan.

'Crying,' said Mary. 'Hungry babies: listen.'

There were no foxes to be heard: only the skillock of birds on Wassand Fell, and the calling of lambs that had gone to the wrong sheep for milk, and been knocked over for thieving. Another sound came from the edge of the fell: the tractor was there carrying stone to mend and build higher the wall between Thoradale and Vendale that kept the sheep in as well as marking the summit of the pass.

Nan unrolled ten feet of the wire netting and laid it out on the grass. Mary rolled it flat, running the tricycle tyre along the selvage.

'Don't do any more,' said Daddy. 'That's enough for now.'

The first post hole had the turf taken from it. The hens came up to the old fence to watch. Daddy knelt and began to take stones from the earth. There was no digging to this job; only loosening of stones, and then the tugging of them out by hand. The farther down you went the harder it was: you had to start at the top again continually to dig out large stones that came half across the place where the hole should be and half under a score of otherwise innocent stones still buried.

Nan took the mattock and started a second hole; she took off the turf, nibbled a piece of sorrel; and found that all the stones below were immovable. The third hole was the same, with a small difference: there was a worm in the turf, and a smart black beetle scurried down among the stones. Worms were one thing: Nan thought they were tidy and clever; but beetles were sly and leggy and disgusted her. Mary thought the opposite: she liked to imagine herself living among beetles and polishing their backs and welcoming them home after their journeys; but there are slugs and worms where beetles live: and when she thought of them she had to change her mind quickly to something else entirely.

Daddy's hole grew slowly. The stones came out moist one by one: each had time to dry to grey speckled with golden powder before the next stone fell beside it.

Mary finished rolling the wire flat. Nan tied her ribbon on again. Daddy snapped his thumbnail on a stone and sandpapered it smooth on a matchbox.

'I think we'll go and help Charley,' said Nan.

'Yes,' said Mary. 'I want to catch a lizard and let it live in my tricycle. It couldn't get out, could it?'

'Hadn't you better go in and see whether Mother wants you for anything?' said Daddy.

'She won't,' said Nan. 'Our hands are dirty.'

'Egg van,' said Mary.

'Washing up,' said Daddy.

'Beds,' said Nan. 'And all sorts of things. Come on, Mary, give me a lift.'

They both rode back to the house on the tricycle. Mother was glad to see them. 'Washing up,' she said.

That was a matter fairly quickly dealt with; but gritty on the whole: Mary saw the cat on the window ledge chattering its jaws at a sparrow above; she threw the wet soap at the cat, and left a lathery mark on its fur. The cat ran away to sleep in a safe place on Lew Scar. Mary went

out and found the soap under the caterpillar-covered nasturtiums, and it had to be washed up with the plates.

'We've got our hands clean,' said Nan.

'Mine aren't very,' said Mary. 'I've only been drying.' Nan washed the tea towel.

The next important thing was the eggs. The egg van came on Saturdays: the eggs had all to be counted and put in their trays in the boxes, and labelled so that the marketer would know they came from Mr Owland of Lew Farm, Thoradale. It was the van's last visit of the week: Lew Farm was the highest in the dale; although it was nearer Vendale no one would take eggs up or down Yowncorn Screw.

Nan wrote the labels: Mary was not always sure which end a word began. 'All the words are different,' she said. 'They don't teach words at school, except ones you don't have, like Minim and Substractors.'

'Words remind you of things,' said Nan: though she had never heard the word before, Substractors reminded her of Algebra; and she had some to look at and do. They were easy sums, but the explanations were ridiculous and full of words that had no meaning at all:

> The middle term has for its coefficient the sum of the numerical quantities (taken with the proper signs) in the second terms of the two binomial expressions;

but the sums belonging to the rigmarole could be done in your head. She wrote the answers in her rough note book. As soon as she had finished Daddy came in looking for somebody to hold the posts whilst he filled in the holes.

Nan held the first post upright. Mary dropped stones back into the hole; Daddy banged them down with the end of the second post, until the hole was almost full. There were stones left over: they would be used to hold down the bottom edge of the netting; Daddy still had to dig a trench to bury a foot of the wire to stop the foxes burrowing their way in underneath. The second post was banged in with the help of the third post.

'Shall I pull the first post out, to bang the last one in with?' asked Nan.

'Of course,' said Daddy. 'Don't break it.'

Mary laughed and dropped a stone on her foot instead

of into the third hole. 'Don't fill the hole with tears,' said Daddy. 'The post will float away.'

He pushed the stones down with his heel. Mary did a

quick two-wheeled in-and-out round the posts; and Mother called them in to dinner.

They waved to Charley, who was sitting on the skyline drinking cold tea, and went in.

All through dinner Daddy was drawing something on a piece of paper. Nan looked at it upside down; Mary looked at it right way up: but there was no making out what it was.

'Won't work,' said Daddy at last, putting his plate on the picture. 'They were dipping sheep years ago, farther down the dale. There was a fox in the middle of the flock, keeping very low, because he could see no way out: there were men all round waiting to catch him at the last.'

'How did he get in?' asked Mary. 'Was he dressed in a lambskin?'

'You're thinking of the grapes and the raven,' said Nan, muddling up Æsop's fables.

'Nobody knows how he got in. But he sat there all day silently, with the sheep taking no notice of him: and one by one they were pulled out from the flock, and dipped, and ducked, and set free.'

'Go on,' said Nan. 'What happened?'

'End of the day,' said Daddy. 'Everybody tired; a dozen sheep in the fold: a dozen men round them. Fox sees his way out. Takes his turn at the gate. Farmer grabs him; hurls him into the dip; they duck him; push him out; and let him go.'

'What happened in the end?' said Nan.

'No fox in the fold,' said Daddy. 'Mystery all round: so they blame the man at the gate.'

"T isn't true,' said Mary.

'Maybe not,' said Daddy. 'But it's an old story.'

'It isn't what you drew,' said Nan.

'I was inventing a fox trap,' said Daddy. 'But it's no good.' He lifted the plate and finished the drawing by adding a laughing fox.

'It would have been funnier if the fox had been clipped with the sheep,' said Mary. 'Can I keep a fox if I find one?'

'You're not to find one,' said Mother, because if she said

yes Mary would bring in any sort of animal instead and leave it in the kitchen and say it would do instead of a fox; if Mother said no, Mary would do the same and point out that it wasn't a fox.

Mary said nothing now. She left her dinner and went to talk to Charley.

'She hasn't gone to Yowncorn Yat, has she?' said Daddy.

'She'll be eating Charley's dinner for him,' said Mother. 'Will you fetch her back, Nan, in case we forget her?'

'She won't go to the Yat alone,' said Nan. 'She knows about the hounds.'

'That's only a tale,' said Daddy. 'It's mine shafts I'm thinking of, and the Dig. The shaft is just the other side of a wall, between here and the Yat. But I can keep an eye on her when I'm putting up the wire.'

Nan went out with him to watch the trench for the wire being dug; but Daddy suggested some weeding.

'The runner beans under the stairs, and the onions in the parlour are the worst,' he said. 'And there's some bind-weed in the hall.'

Daddy had long ago puzzled out why the farm garden was so neat, with such narrow paths with gaps in them: the garden had once been a house. Now the bottom two feet only of the house were left, and each room was full of black soil that would grow anything. The foundations of the house were laid out in plan, and each bed was called something: hall, scullery, parlour; even a kitchen cup-board where Mary grew fossils and ants and campanulas and buried dead birds.

Nan did a considerable routing out of soft thistles and braids of bindweed with silent swinging white bells. She took an armful out over the parlour wall and threw all the green to the hens. Daddy had dug his trench now; she went to hold the netting for him whilst he tacked it to the post with staples. The wire stood upright in a silver screen between her and Daddy.

Mary, two hundred feet higher, half in Thoradale and half in Vendale, sitting astride the wall talking to Charley and teasing a rove beetle that she thought was a scorpion hidden in a hole, saw the white zinc coat of the netting sparking sunlight up from the green field, and left Charley and the chinking walling hammer. Charley with his head over the stones he was shaping went on talking to her: but only the rove beetle heard; and the little foxes laughed under Yowncorn Yat.

Mary found Nan and Daddy walking on either side of the wire, pacing to and fro thoughtfully like two caged bears measuring each other up for a fight.

'We're treading the grass down again,' said Nan. 'We've buried the wire, you see.'

'Good heavens,' said Daddy, 'milking time.'

'Nan,' said Mary, 'you look like a jigsaw puzzle.'

'So I do,' said Nan, holding out her hand. She was patterned all over with the shadow of the six-sided mesh.

'You look as if you'd been knitted,' said Daddy. Then he shouted for Charley.

'He won't hear,' said Mary. 'He's the other side of the wall, talking to me.'

'I'll go up,' said Nan. 'He can bring me down on the tractor.'

Mary went up with her, considering that there would be a ride. Charley looked up from his stone chipping surprised at the gone afternoon and stiff from being so long bent. He left the tractor where it was, and ran down the two intakes to the farm.

'We shall have to walk down,' said Nan.

'Let's go and look at something,' said Mary.

'Not the Yat,' said Nan, thinking about mine shafts and hounds.

'No. Something green,' said Mary. 'In Vendale.'

They were at the top of the pass now. When they looked back Thoradale could be clearly seen, particularly the farm and the house plan of the garden: ahead there was still a couple of furlongs of rough pasture before any more of Vendale could be seen than Horse Head on the other side, and, a whole dale beyond, Pen-y-ghent.

From the next wall but one they saw Yowncorn Screw ahead and below. To the left there was dominant Yowncorn Yat; below the Yat was the side of Vendale and the top of the long furrow in the ground called the Dig. They were about halfway along Vendale at this point, and they could see a little way up it, and a little way down it.

Mary wanted to look at something immediately below and in front.

'See,' she said. 'I thought so.'

'It's all fairly green,' said Nan.

'Only a window and a door,' said Mary. 'The Unicorn

Inn, I mean. That Grammar School prefect has been painting it.'

'I don't suppose *he* has,' said Nan. 'He probably brought
the paint from somewhere for someone. Come on: we'd
better go back for tea.'

'Listen,' said Mary. 'Foxes.'

There was nothing to be heard but the birds and the
sheep, and the water falling down the Dig.

'Not even enough wind to squeak the signboard,' said
Nan.

A long time later, when Charley had brought the
tractor down and gone home, and the farm was in twilight
under the fells, the egg van came. Nan and Mary rode up
to the bank in it, to open the gate and get to bed after the
usual time. When the gate was closed after him, the van

driver waved to them, and they stood on the bars to wave back. The van helter-skeltered down the Bank.

'Look,' said Mary. Out of Vendale and the sunset came a cyclist. He wore a Grammar School cap with the prefects' red ring; he had a stripe of green paint on his right cheek, and his blazer had one green sleeve.

Mary waved to him as he went past. He waved back, saw Nan on the gate, almost stopped; and went on again.

'You shouldn't wave to *him*,' said Nan, when he had gone down into the shadow. 'He isn't a prefect: he's the Head Boy. He's next to the Headmaster. That's Forrest. He nearly came back and told me not to be so cheeky about letting you wave to him.'

Mary changed the subject. 'Listen,' she said. 'Foxes.'

On Wassand Fell a cub saw the sunset and yapped. In answer the sun sent a last red flame on to Yowncorn Yat.

CHAPTER THREE

STORY TELLING

Daddy stopped the car at the top of Yowncorn Screw. He always did; to make sure he went slowly enough down the twists.

The road dropped two hundred feet in quarter of a mile. The heavy air filled Nan's ears and made them buzz. She swallowed; her ears clicked: and they were clear again; and she heard the water dropping down the Dig: two hundred feet in a furlong: twice as steeply as the road.

They crossed the water of the Dig. Everyone looked up at the mouth of the eroded scar on the hill. The white water hurled itself down the shadow.

'Much too easy to be drowned there,' said Daddy in a warning way: there was a story about the man who had let the water free in the Dig; once there had been no water at all.

'Green paint,' said Mary. They were at the bottom of the Screw now, about to join the road that ran up Vendale. The Unicorn Inn stood above the junction, facing the hillside. New paint shone in the sunlight; and on a ladder against an upstair window stood the painter. Part of him could not be seen, because the signboard with its faded Unicorn was close beside his right arm.

'Our Head Boy,' said Nan. 'Forrest.'

'Perhaps he's related to Mildred Dyson,' said Mother.
'There she is. Give her a wave, Nan: she won't see me.'

Nan waved to Mrs Dyson, who was standing at the foot
of the ladder.

'Didn't see,' said Nan. 'But there's Peter, sitting on the
wall.'

'Not helping with the painting?' said Mother. 'Not like
Peter.'

Mary looked out of the back window at Peter sitting
alone on the garden wall of the Inn. 'Somebody's cross
with him,' she said. 'Or he's cross with them.' Mary was
an expert on Peter, because they went to school together
each day.

'I don't see how you could tell that from an inspection
lasting two seconds,' said Daddy.

They drove two miles down Vendale, and came to Wassand with the church bells ringing above them, and went to church.

After church Daddy was going to look at some pigs higher up the dale. Nobody wanted to go with him, so he left them at the junction before the Unicorn Inn and went on alone.

'Don't you be cheeky to Forrest,' said Nan to Mary.

'I'm not frightened of him,' said Mary.

'Nor am I,' said Nan, but that was not true. 'I don't think he'd speak to us anyway.'

Peter Dyson had left the garden wall. Nan and Mary and Mother went to the Inn door, with the black notice above saying: 'Mildred Dyson. Licensed to sell Beer, Ales, Wines, and Tobacco, to be consumed on or off the Premises.'

Mother went in, with a glance upwards first to the boy on top of the ladder, in case of splashes of paint. Nan went in with her. Mary stood to one side of the door, to avoid having the signboard between her and the boy, and said: 'Hello, Forrest.'

'Mary,' said Nan, snatching at one of Mary's pigtails, but not daring to come out of the doorway. She knew it was wrong for Mary to say 'Forrest' like that. 'Mr Forrest' sounded wrong as well. 'Say "Master Forrest".'

'Hello, Master Forrest,' said Mary, pulling the pigtail away from Nan.

'Hello, Miss Owland,' said the boy, when he had finished his brush stroke.

'Mary,' said Mary.

'Come inside,' said Nan. 'And shut up.' Mary had no idea of the proper way to speak to a Head Boy: he would think they were a very bad-mannered family altogether. Even the Headmaster himself, if he wanted to speak to Forrest, said: 'Can you spare me a moment, Forrest?' And Forrest said: 'I'd like to finish this map, Sir. Will half past twelve do?' And the Headmaster said: 'Yes, Forrest.' Nan had heard that exact conversation.

Forrest began to come down the ladder. Nan went in and closed the door.

Mother and Mrs Dyson were talking about hearthrugs in the kitchen; and drinking cups of tea.

'Hello, Nan,' said Mrs Dyson. 'Will you tell Adam there's a cup of tea for him?'

'Adam?' asked Nan.

'Adam Forrest,' said Mrs Dyson. 'He's just outside: you know him quite well. He was asking about you last night.'

'About me?' said Nan. 'What for?'

'What you were like,' said Mrs Dyson. 'But tell him I've poured his tea.'

'Can't Peter?' said Nan, dreading the idea of having to start a conversation with Forrest. What if he turned round and said: 'Take your sister away, Owland, and don't let me see it again'?

Peter was sitting against the kitchen range, in the fender, with the dog's head in his lap.

'Our Hewlin's off to sleep,' he said.

'Go on, Nan,' said Mother.

Nan went out again. Forrest and Mary were coming in through the door. Forrest bent his head under the low lintel. Mary was holding his hand and talking to him about a painting book she had. 'He must think we're an unbrainy family,' thought Nan. Forrest saw her.

'Hello, Owland,' he said.

'Please, Forrest,' said Nan. 'Mrs Dyson's got some tea poured for you.'

'Forrest is only his school name,' said Mary. 'He's really Adam.'

'Yes, I am,' said Forrest. 'Look, Owland, will you bring my cup of tea outside? I want to talk to you.'

'Yes, Forrest,' said Nan, not wanting to be talked to by him: and not daring to disobey.

'Adam,' he said.

'Adam, I mean,' said Nan, feeling as cheeky as a mosquito.

'And bring young Peter,' said Adam. He went out again with Mary. Nan went back to the kitchen for the cup of tea. Peter shook his head when she asked him to come.

'He's shy,' said Mrs Dyson. 'Won't go near him. We haven't heard yet whether Peter's passed the exam for the school.'

'He's sure to ask me,' said Peter. 'And what if I didn't pass after all?' He sat tighter against the stove, and would not move.

Nan took the cup of tea out into the sunshine. Adam was sitting on the bench beside the door.

'Thank you,' he said. 'Nan, isn't it? Is Peter coming?'

27

'He won't,' said Nan.

'He hasn't come near me at all,' said Adam. 'But I can't talk to you without him.'

'I'll get him,' said Mary. She left Nan alone with Adam.

'I didn't stop last night, because I hadn't much life left in the lamp battery,' said Adam. 'And I wasn't certain it was you: so I only waved to Mary.'

Mary came back dragging Hewlin; Peter followed: he thought he could get away if he wanted.

'Hello, Peter,' said Adam. 'Come and sit down.'

'He'll be all right, you know,' said Mary. 'I told him about you. He was frightened of you.'

'All the juniors are,' said Adam. 'But I never say anything to any of them, because I can't remember their names. Don't tell them that, will you, Nan?'

They all sat on the bench, with Hewlin at the end resting his yellow face on Peter's shoulder.

'Oh, shift off, Hewlin,' said Peter. Mary knew that he meant he was pleased at being sent for by Adam, and not so awestruck.

'Now,' said Adam. 'Somebody tell me about the hounds and the Unicorn, and the gateway, and everything.'

'It's a legend,' said Nan. 'A tale. It might not be true.'

'There's some story about the Yat,' said Adam. 'Yowncorn Yat means Unicorn Gate, but what is the story?'

'Foxes,' said Mary. 'Baby brown foxes.'

'That isn't the story,' said Nan. 'Why did you ask us, Forrest—I mean, Adam?'

'Well, why, Nan?'

'I do know,' said Nan. 'It's because it's our family in the legend.'

'And mine,' said Peter. 'Mary and I are cousins.'

'Sort of, you are,' said Nan.

'Tell me about it,' said Adam.

'Daddy would know better,' said Nan, in case she got it wrong.

'Yes,' said Adam. 'But I know you; and Peter's mother is sort of my cousin, so I know him: you're the best people to ask.'

'It was all a long time ago,' said Nan. 'It was our ancestor who went to a Crusade, or a war.'

'We grow onions in his parlour,' said Mary.

Nan explained about the garden at Lew Farm.

'That'll be interesting,' said Adam. 'Go on.'

'He was a Sir somebody,' said Nan. 'He had a beautiful daughter called Gertrude. He had to go off to see the king, when he got back from the war; and there was an inn here, but I don't know what it was called. The man at the inn here wanted to marry Gertrude, but Sir Owland wouldn't let him. He brought a unicorn from abroad, and trained it for hunting, and he got a pack of savage dogs.'

'Oh, shift off, Hewlin,' said Peter. 'Our Hewlin was one of them.'

'Yes?', said Adam, not sure what Peter meant.

'The man from the inn went to Lew Farm, when Sir Owland had gone, but the dogs . . .'

'Hounds,' said Mary.

'Hounds were all round, and he couldn't get in: and the unicorn tried to spear him with his spear.'

'So he went away,' said Mary. 'And got magic.'

'That's true,' said Peter. 'That's how I got Hewlin.'

'Nobody would help him,' said Nan. 'He had to get magic, and the magic sent all the dogs into Yowncorn Yat, and the unicorn too, and they go running round Fairyland under Wassand Fell.'

'They didn't take our Hewlin,' said Peter.

'Be quiet, Peter,' said Nan. 'Then the man went to the farm, and took Gertrude away, and they were married in Wassand church, and lived in this inn, and Sir Owland wouldn't come back from London.'

'Frightened of magic,' said Mary.

'No,' said Nan. 'He laughed and laughed until he died of it.'

'Why?' asked Adam.

'Because all his money was fastened to the hounds' collars, and to the unicorn, and when they were lost all the money was lost too.'

'All lost but two faithful faithful dogs,' said Peter. 'One was Hewlin, weren't you, my honey?' Hewlin licked his face.

'Two dogs escaped,' said Nan. 'One faithfully stopped with Gertrude. It was deaf, you see; and the other didn't get into Fairyland, and it stayed on the Fell; and Hewlin is descended from them. It comes back sometimes, doesn't it, Peter?'

'They say,' said Peter. 'But our Hewlin's got his own name and his own collar. Look: that's treasure.'

He unbuckled Hewlin's collar and handed it to Adam.

'What is it?' said Adam, taking the collar.

It was an inch wide leather strap, with a buckle and a disk saying: 'Dyson, Unicorn Inn, Wassand, Vendale.'

'Not so much need to look at the leather,' said Peter. 'That's a new bit. See the outside of the collar.'

Sewn on the outside with gut there was a silver chain, with thick links, some of them broken. At one end there was a silver catch, and at the other a silver hook. The metal was all black now: Adam only saw the white gleam when he rubbed the tarnish away with his handkerchief.

'Treasure,' said Peter. 'Come here, Hewlin, you. You can't go without it.'

'I didn't know that,' said Adam. 'Nan, why did only a deaf dog escape, and one other.'

'It didn't hear the fairies,' said Mary. 'And the other one was lame and the gate was closed when it got there.'

'Like Hamelin,' said Adam.

'That's right,' said Nan. 'They were hunting-dogs: hounds, you see; and the fairies blew a hunting horn, and they went to follow the hunt.'

'And they're still at it, going round and round under Wassand Fell, unicorn and all,' said Peter. 'They went in through the Yat.'

'And what about the Dig, up there?' said Adam. 'What's that to do with it?'

'Dyson's dig,' said Peter. 'Ratty little foxes live there, don't they, Hewlin? It was that Dyson that married Gertrude Owland, trying to get back in and get at the treasure.'

'But he didn't, I suppose,' said Adam.

'Not him,' said Peter. 'See all that water?'

'I should think so,' said Adam, looking up at the white tongue licking the rocky gradient.

'When he got nigh the gate,' said Peter, 'the fairies opened up the beck inside, and sent him down drowned. It washed him to Wassand churchyard, and they buried him there: so they never got the treasure—only what our Hewlin's got.'

'We'll get the rest,' said Adam.

Mr Owland drove up from Vendale then, and blew his horn to bring Mother out.

'I must finish that window before dinner,' said Adam. 'Do you think it looks better, Peter?'

'I do,' said Peter. 'Shift off, Hewlin.'

Mother came out of the inn with Mrs Dyson. Peter and Hewlin went in.

'I'll see you tomorrow, Nan,' said Adam, with one foot on the ladder.

'We'll come this afternoon,' said Nan. 'It's such a fine day.'

'Good,' said Adam. 'If you remember anything else, tell me.'

Daddy felt all the doors of the car to make sure they were fastened, and charged at the Screw: you came down as slowly as you could and went up as fast as you could.

'Oh, Mother,' said Mary. 'That was Adam.'

'We're going to find Sir Owland's lost dogs and the treasure,' said Nan.

'You couldn't take it from the fairies,' said Mary.

'Wait and see,' said Nan. But she had no idea what Adam meant to do about fairies. Perhaps the fifth form learnt about things like that.

'Don't eat anything in Fairyland,' said Mother. 'That's the only rule I know.'

CHAPTER FOUR

A STRANGE SIGN

In the afternoon clouds came floating on a low tide of wind, grounded on Wassand Fell, and sank into the heather. The hill appeared without a top: over Thoradale the sky was close and white.

'Rain before morning,' said Daddy.

'We'll take our coats this afternoon,' said Nan.

'If we get there,' said Mary.

'Take them before you start,' said Mother. 'And why shouldn't you get there, and where is it?'

Nan explained that they were going back to the Unicorn to talk about the lost hounds and their silver collars.

'You've to come home for tea,' said Mother.

'I thought we might get lost on the way,' said Mary. 'It's such a lovely day, you see.'

'What you think of it depends on your trade,' said Daddy. 'Can you find hounds better in the rain?'

'I can find a lot of things,' said Mary. She was unable to explain how hopeful you could be in a mist; how you might find yourself in some sunny unknown land where everything was understood, and the things you had always wanted were there waiting for you to take them.

'Maryland,' said Mother: she knew Mary's thoughts.

Nan took with her two bottles that had held Dandelion

34

and Burdock: there was twopence back on each of them. Mary took nothing but a farthing: that is what a pedlar or a packman wants for his valuable wares.

'Don't come back covered with paint,' said Mother.

They went straight up the gable of the dale, over the intakes, towards the clouds. At the top the only thing seen certainly was Thoradale; every tree and wall was bright and distinct and solid and silent: in all its green length nothing moved but the silent cows. The lambs were none of them lost and noisy; the birds closed their beaks and stayed under the bushes. The whole dale lay lapped in cloud and sleep.

Towards Vendale nothing could be seen. The cloud licked over the walls and hid the intakes: there was nothing to fix your eyes on; the sheep tracks were the only guide.

At the second wall they left the world behind, and all they had was the patch of ground where they walked. As they went down hill, first their feet left the cloud, and then their knees, and the rest of them gradually. Mary was first out, disappointed to find ahead only Vendale: she had hoped for her new strange land.

Nan looked down at the Unicorn Inn.

'He does get on,' she said.

'He isn't so very slow,' said Mary. 'Let's run.'

They ran down among the sheep, crossed the Screw twice, and then came on to it again to cross the waters of Dyson's Dig. The water cascaded from the cloud like melting mist; and the loud shout of each flying fall was reflected back from the white roof above.

'We'd better walk,' said Nan. She began to feel shy of Adam again, as if he might know she had not copied her Algebra neatly, nor touched the French book to find out reflexive perfects, and not bothered her Latin book at all about second-declension adjectives.

Mary had none of these things to think of. She ran ahead to see what Adam was doing now.

He was at the foot of the ladder, confessing a mistake to Peter and Hewlin. He was washing paint brushes in turpentine.

'I've run out of paint,' he said. 'I've used much more than I thought I should.'

'The inn looks very nice,' said Nan: she felt that some-one who made mistakes himself would not ask her about homework.

'It looks brighter,' said Adam. 'And now I think I might as well go home, and come back better prepared tomorrow evening.'

'Oh no,' said Mary. 'You must stay.'

'Our Hewlin will get you a rabbit, if you've done painting,' said Peter.

Hewlin was a ramshackle dog. He wagged his tail and himself so hard that his hind feet left the ground, and he sat down suddenly.

'He's got a green ear,' said Peter. 'He's the colour of grass; the rabbits won't see him coming.'

'Don't catch a rabbit,' said Mary. She always hoped that a rabbit would one day invite her into its burrow; and how could it invite anybody who went rabbiting with Hewlin?

'No R in the month,' said Adam. 'Besides, I've that idea about something else: but I haven't asked your mother yet.'

'Oh, that,' said Peter. 'You ask her: she won't mind. Here, come by, Hewlin. No rabbits today, my honey.'

'We shall want a rope,' said Adam. 'Not a thick one.'

'You go off then and ask her,' said Peter. 'She won't mind so very much. I'll get a rope.'

Adam stepped over Hewlin, who was lying on his yellow back licking Peter's shoe. Adam put the cleaned brushes on the bench, and went into the inn.

'He can do it like anything,' said Peter. 'His father builds houses and paints them.'

'What's he going to do next, then?' asked Nan.

'The signboard,' said Peter. 'It's what he wants to do, but he held off asking our mum: she might have said against it. But he can draw, just like writing—easy.'

'I can draw better than write,' said Mary.

'He's the best at drawing in the school,' said Nan. 'Not Mary's sort of drawing, but real things.'

'She can draw more than you,' said Peter. He always took Mary's side.

'Of course I can,' said Mary.

'That's made you think,' said Peter.

To stop their arguments Nan gave them one of the empty Dandelion and Burdock bottles between them. Peter took her own as well, and brought back fourpence. He gave Nan a penny, and Mary a penny, and when Adam came out gave him another, and kept one himself.

'What's it for?' asked Adam.

'Empty bottles,' said Mary. 'You can have mine too: I've got some money already.' She thought a farthing was the most you ought to carry about with you.

'Can you do it, Adam?' asked Peter.

'Yes,' said Adam. 'She's very pleased. So am I. The first thing is to get the board down: I can paint it best in the stable. There's plenty of light, and it doesn't matter if it rains.'

Peter went off with Hewlin to find a rope. Adam took the ladder from the window he had finished, and leaned it close against the iron sign bar. The sign moved a little in the wind, and the hinges squeaked like nestlings.

Adam went up the ladder, to see how the sign was hung, and what he would need to bring it down.

'We may find something interesting in this,' he said. 'There may be another picture under this one telling us more about the hounds. I should think this is a pretty old board; but I don't know enough about them to be sure. I say, Nan, you'll find my bicycle just inside the stable door. There's a can of oil in the saddlebag.'

'I'll get it,' said Nan. She found it, unscrewed the cap on the spout, and handed the can to Adam. He put oil on the inner hinge, then leaned over and anointed the outer one. He swung the board; its squeak grew at once angry, and then faded away to a smooth grumble.

'All I have to do is knock out a couple of pins,' said Adam. 'I'll lash the sign up, so that it won't fall down, get the pins out, and then you can lower it gently down on a rope. We might find the clue to the hound business when we've cleaned it up a bit.'

'What could we find?' asked Nan. 'There could hardly be anything on the signboard. All it said was: "Unicorn Inn. Free House." written below the rampant unicorn. Above the beast his horn went up into a corner; and there was a reminder of the rest of the legend above: the top of the board was shaped like a hunting horn; with a broad bell and a narrow end where you might blow. All seemed to be carved from one piece of wood: all was painted black.

Peter came back with a rope. 'Clothes line,' he said. 'Make haste with it, or our mum will be on at us if she sees.'

'We shan't waste time,' said Adam. 'Have you a hammer, Peter?'

When Peter came back with the hammer, Adam had lashed the signboard up with the clothes line under the projecting ends of the board, where it was shaped like a hunting horn. He let the ends of the rope fall to the ground. Mary held them.

'Don't pull,' he said. 'This is a highwayman's knot: one end to undo the lashing, and the other to lower with.' He came down a little way for the hammer, blew the coal dust off it, and began to tap the pins from the hinges.

The first one fell to the stones below. Hewlin sniffed at it. The second pin fell: the signboard sagged into the ropes. Hewlin examined the second pin, and sat down to wait for more.

'Pull one rope,' said Adam. 'I don't know which is which.'

Nan pulled; but that rope was tight. Mary pulled the other: it jerked in her hands and came loose. Nan felt the weight of the board on the other rope.

'Slowly,' said Adam. He steadied the board, and it began to come down. He jumped off the ladder and lowered the board to the ground.

'I thought so,' said Mrs Dyson. She had come out with an armful of wet tea towels.

'I'll put it back,' said Peter. 'We've only taken it for a minute.' Nan wound the rope over her hand and elbow; Mary took the peg bag; Adam took the wet cloths; Peter led the way into the garden; and they hung the cloths out to dry.

'Well, thank you,' said Mrs Dyson. 'I think my hands were the cleanest, after all.'

'Never mind,' said Mary. 'Daddy says it's going to rain.'

Hewlin was watching over the signboard.

'Come by, Hewlin,' said Peter. 'Shift off.'

Adam pulled the board up, and took it into the stable. There were no horses now; only Mrs Dyson's bicycle and the ancient dust. Hewlin came in to dream of rats; and sat his yellow self down in the black fallen cobwebs.

Adam put the signboard on two trestles. 'We'd better dust it,' he said.

'Soap and water,' said Nan. 'Scrub it.'

'I'll ask our mum,' said Peter. 'I mustn't make her tatchy.'

Mrs Dyson provided three scrubbing brushes. Mary acted as soapholder, and pointed out patches that had been missed. When they had finished scrubbing, the board was covered with soap lather. Adam fetched clean water and rinsed the soap away.

'Now,' he said. 'Can anybody see anything useful?'

The signboard glistened in the cloudlight: but the longer they looked at it the dryer it became, and the duller it grew.

'No different from what it was,' said Adam.

'What do you think it will do?' asked Mary: half expecting the unicorn to move its head and speak.

'It's an old bit of wood,' said Adam. 'It might have something helpful on it. I hope I find something there. The Headmaster made a bet with me that I wouldn't find out all about the hounds. I told him what I was going to do, you see.'

'Are you going to take him the treasure?' asked Nan.

'Yes,' said Adam.

'Is there a magic word written on the board?' asked Mary. 'Do you know what they mean?'

'There may be a word written on it,' said Adam. 'But it isn't magic. We don't bother about such things nowadays.'

'We do,' said Mary.

'Oh well, little girls do, but not anybody else,' said Adam. 'How could they?'

'But we *told* you about the magic,' said Mary. 'It must be true.'

'It isn't,' said Adam. 'There isn't any.'

'But if your Headmaster said there was, then there must be.'

'He didn't say there was,' said Adam. 'He said it was only a story, but I said it might be true. But nobody really thinks there's magic in it.'

'I shall hate you, that's all,' said Mary. 'I thought you were nice, but you aren't.'

'You shouldn't argue with her,' said Nan. 'Now she's crying.'

'Always at it,' said Peter. He would have nothing to do with Mary if she cried. 'Roaring like all that.'

Mary's tears were soon gone. She dried them away with her handkerchief, and, since she had it in her hand, she began to dry up a few drops of water on the signboard.

'Is this writing?' she said. She was drying the bell of the hunting horn. 'There's something shining underneath the paint.'

Adam bent to look: there was a gleam of metal on the rim of the bell.

'End of a brass nail, I should think,' he said. 'Sign's made of oak, I expect, and you never use iron nails in oak.' He took out his knife and scratched the paint. The blade uncovered a patch of dark wood; then it drew off a straight-edged flake of paint. Under the paint there was dirty brass, brown and green, but bright where the knife had marked it.

'Just a band to hold the wood together,' said Adam. He scratched again, and this time a larger flake fell, and left an engraved letter still full of black paint, an N.

'Go on,' said Nan. 'Go on.'

'Magic,' said Mary, feeling at the same time triumph and sorrow for her enemies.

'Hmn,' said Adam, seeing the fancy looking like a fact. He scratched again.

'H, E, W, L, I, N,' said Peter. 'Our Hewlin. Come by, you.' Hewlin came up to see his name.

'Well I never,' said Adam. 'I wonder if there's anything the other side.'

'Turn it over,' said Nan. Adam turned the signboard over, and went to the other side of the trestle. He scraped again.

'B, E, L, A, N, T, E, R,' said Nan. 'No such word.'

'That there is,' said Peter. 'It means if you are late somewhere. That'll be the name of the hound that didn't get into the Fell. If Hewlin's one on 'em, Belanter's t'other. Belanter. I didn't know it was called that.'

Adam scraped the rest of the inch-wide rounded rim. There was nothing else engraved on it.

'Well?' said Mary.

Adam looked at her. 'Just put on to remember them by,' he said. He was saved from saying the wrong thing to Mary: a car stopped outside and Mary went to see whether it was Daddy.

'We're late,' said Nan. 'We're supposed to be home for tea.'

'You're belantered,' said Peter.

Mary came in to tell Nan to come at once.

'I'll see you tomorrow,' said Adam. 'We'll have a really good look at this picture.'

Daddy looked at all four of the car doors. He started the engine and they charged up the Screw and into the clouds.

'It's thick on top,' he said. 'I thought I'd save you the walk round the road. What are you scowling about, Mary?'

'I don't want to go to the Grammar School,' said Mary. 'It's a funny school if they don't learn about stories.'

CHAPTER FIVE

AN ECHO FAIRY

Nan rode down the dale on Monday morning with Charley; single file over Lew Gill and along Thora Beck.

'Not so very long before we bring t' sheep in to clip,' said Charley.

'I did twelve last year,' said Nan. 'But I wish they didn't smell so strong.'

'Nay, they smell grand,' said Charley. 'But happen Ah like t' smell o' t' old cows better.'

'It's a good thing we don't have to clip cows,' said Nan. 'I shouldn't earn anything at that.'

'Do it wi' a scythe,' said Charley. 'Happen tha'd tomahawk off t' lugs and t' tail.'

'Do the sheep clipping on a Saturday, then,' said Nan. 'I always like some extra money.'

Charley went to his house for breakfast; Nan rode on beside the beck until she came to the road and the school where Mary and Peter went. She left her bicycle there, and waited for the bus to Thornton.

When Nan got off the bus that afternoon, Adam was there on his bicycle, hot with work.

'I just did it,' he said. 'I got a pull up on a lorry. Then I followed the bus until you got off.'

'I'll show you the way I go,' said Nan. 'Not over the Bank, but along the Beck.'

When they got to Lew Farm they were still in the bottom of the valley. 'I'll have to go up all the same,' said Adam. 'And it seems to be steeper up your lane than it is up the Bank itself.'

'You can leave your bicycle here,' said Nan. 'You can't ride up this side, and you can't ride down the other, so you have to walk both ways in any case.'

Mary was waiting at the plank bridge for them: she could come no farther on the tricycle. Nan rode across at once, though the plank was wet from rain. Adam thought about the plank, and came across delicately, expecting to be skidded off into the Gill.

'It's been raining a lot of the time,' said Mary. 'And it's been dark all day. I caught a frog.' She showed them a big toad in the tray of the tricycle. Nan told her what it was, and after that Mary refused to touch it. Nan lifted it out and put it in a stony house Mary had made, with a little damp paper notice over the door: 'FRAG'; the toad sat there with its jewelled eyes staring on either side.

'Oh well,' said Mary. 'I know it liked having a ride. It got bigger and bigger.'

'It puffed itself angrily full of air,' said Nan.

Adam put his bicycle next to the tractor. 'I'll go on,' he said. 'Are you coming now or after?'

'After,' said Nan. 'Homework first, then tea, then washing up, then more homework. Then I'll come.'

'We ought to be able to deal with the homework,' said Adam.

'Geometry and Geography,' said Nan.

They went indoors to see what could be done about finishing it quickly. Mary came in to look; the Geometry was lines and letters. 'What does it do?' she asked.

'Oh, nothing,' said Nan. 'You just learn it. But I'm good at the stuff, so I don't mind.'

The Geography was a map of Africa. Mary knew something about maps and plans: the farm garden was a plan. 'Where is that place?' she wanted to know.

Adam pointed to the south and east. Mary shook her head. 'That's Vendale,' she said.

'The other side of Vendale,' said Adam. 'Black people live there.'

'Oh, *I* know,' said Mary, satisfied that Geography was a useful sort of story. 'Redskins.' She went outside and thought herself out a conversation with a black Redskin who walked out of a cloud on Wassand Fell. 'The little foxes,' he said, 'have nothing to eat. Their names are. . . .'

Adam came out, because the Geometry was done, and the Geography well under way. Mary woke out of her thought.

'He was just going to tell me their names,' she said.

'Who was?' said Adam.

'The foxes' names,' said Mary. 'He won't tell me now, and I shall never know. But that doesn't matter, because I know the name of the lost dog.'

'Belanter,' said Adam. 'Yes, we know that.'

'They'll tell us whether they let him in if we ask them', said Mary. 'But we mustn't eat anything, or they'll keep us for seven years. But if we call him he'll come back.'

'How?' said Adam. 'What will he come back for?'

'From being lost, because we know his name,' said Mary. 'You always have to know their names. But you came out just when I was going to know the foxes' names.'

'I must go to the inn,' said Adam. He stepped over Mary, and went to his bicycle to collect a small can of green paint and a box of colours for the signboard, as well as some designs he had thought of during the day.

'You can get lost in the clouds, easily,' said Mary.

'I'll take care not to,' said Adam.

Mary went in. Adam had not understood that she thought anyone would like to be lost in a cloud if they could; and that a cloud on a hill was the best place to lose yourself in.

Adam walked up the Bank on to the road.

'That was very hospitable of you,' said Mother to Nan, meaning that it was not. 'You drag him in and make him do your homework, and let him go on without any tea. Did you ask him whether he would have some?'

Nan had thought about it, and decided that she dare not ask the Head Boy to have tea, in case he said no. But Mother had not really minded; the kitchen was very hot today, and full of drying clothes: washing day at Lew Farm took no notice of the weather.

'He could have helped with the washing up,' said Mother. Nan hoped Mother would never suggest such a thing to a Head Boy.

Mary rang the bell from the window. Daddy came in for his tea.

'Any more news of the silver collars?' he asked.

'Nothing,' said Nan. 'We found the hounds' names; and that's all: there isn't anything else; but Forrest thinks he might find another picture under the one that's on now.'

'It's a very old trail to follow,' said Daddy. 'I don't think you'll find the answer. Don't you go digging up my vegetables in search of clues, will you?'

'But why would they put the name on the sign?' said Nan.

'Forty or fifty years ago there used to be hare hunting,

on foot with harriers,' said Daddy. 'Just the sort of hunting they've had for hundreds of years: everybody had a dog or two—harriers, they were—and when anybody felt like hunting, all he did was blow a horn, and if you couldn't go yourself you let your hounds go all the same, and they'd go straight for the horn, and then to find a hare, and chase him for miles. Sometimes they'd get a fox instead.'

'But still, why have the names written on the signboard?'

'I don't think anybody will ever know,' said Daddy. 'Perhaps he put it there in memory of them.'

Nan and Mother did the washing up. Mary went out to look at the toad in the house labelled 'FRAG'. He had shrunk down and closed his eyes. Mary tiptoed away, not wanting to wake him up.

'You're to start back at exactly eight o'clock,' said Mother. 'Not a minute later.' Nan put her watch back to agree with the kitchen clock; and left for the inn.

The mist lying in the pass was thinner today: now and then there opened a vista of coarse grass, with perhaps a wall at the end, or a sheep; then a moving berg of mist would roll across and hide all vision.

'It's soaked into the ground,' said Nan. 'Or come down as rain.'

'Making all the animals wet,' said Mary, thinking of a shivering fox and a rain-sprinkled rabbit.

They were on top of the pass, with the mist all round against their eyes. There was a call or cry from far to the left.

'Listen,' said Mary. 'Foxes.'

'A dog,' said Nan. They heard it again: a houndlike half-barking yell. 'Hewlin can't find his rabbit.'

Hewlin was sometimes good at a rabbit, sometimes bad. On a heavy day he could not tell which was a new trail and which was an old one: he howled when he confused himself.

'Lost again,' said Mary. 'Not so very good at hunting in the washy weather.'

'He might have been sniffing at the turpentine, and lost his sense of smell,' said Nan. 'Dogs do.'

The dog howled again, with a sharp sad bark after the howl.

'Quite lost,' said Mary. 'We must find him. He'll be under the Yat.'

'You don't want to go to the Yat,' said Nan. 'Do you? Hadn't we better go to the inn?'

'I don't mind going to the Yat today,' said Mary. 'Really I don't. I'll go alone if you're frightened.'

'I'm not frightened,' said Nan. 'But we'd better look carefully where we walk, especially near walls, because of mineshafts.'

The dog howled continually now; sometimes softly, sometimes loudly, but always from the same place: the far left, under Yowncorn Yat. Nan and Mary turned away from the sheep track through the intakes, and went to the left, the east.

The ground rose slowly, higher to the right: Nan knew the shape of the ground, and that there was a ridge from the foot of the Yat to the intakes.

They went on without talking, across the grass and spongy reeds and between the crusts of green heather. Still the dog barked and howled ahead. There was a wall in front. Nan looked over it: there was no pit beyond. They climbed over, and they were in a little mistless dip, with the wall behind them, close-cropped turf under their feet, and ahead the steep little slopes running up to the Yat.

'Have you been here before?' said Mary.

'I think so,' said Nan quickly: Mary was about to have the idea that they had wandered out of the world.

The dog could not be heard.

'Gone home,' said Mary. 'Oh.'

'Then we can go back,' said Nan.

'I wanted to find the dog,' said Mary.

'We shall find it when we get to the Unicorn,' said Nan. 'He can find his own way about quite easily.'

'No he can't,' said Mary. 'He's lost. Go on, near the Yat. We'll find him there.'

They went on, up the steep little slope to a round crest, with the mist about them again. Once more they heard the dog howling.

'Go on,' said Mary.

'We'd better go round a bit,' said Nan. 'There's a lot of rocks in front: a sort of scar.'

They moved to the right, to the south, and came down the other side of the hillock, over the long ridge they had skirted all the way from the intakes. When they were at the top the dog was calling from the left. But as soon as they had gone twenty feet down the hillside they heard the sound coming distinctly and repeatedly from the right.

'He must run quickly,' said Nan.

'You don't think so very much,' said Mary. 'That's Hewlin you can hear.'

'I know,' said Nan. 'Who did you think it was?'

'The first one was Belanter,' said Mary.

'Rubbish,' said Nan. 'How could it be?'

'It's because we know his name,' said Mary. 'I told you we had to know his name before he would come.'

'It's only one dog,' said Nan.

'Go back to the top, and listen to the other,' said Mary. 'I'll stay here and listen to Hewlin. If Belanter comes to you, you've only got to say his name, and he won't hurt you.'

Nan went up the hill again, wondering how Mary could be right, and what to do if she was. Before she reached the top of the hill the dog called again. This time the noise came from both sides: first from the left, the direction of Vendale and the inn, and immediately an answer from the right, the Yat.

Nan stood still. The dog called again: back came the answer. Mary looked up and smiled.

'Call him,' she said. Nan turned and looked at her, then turned again and went up the hill.

From here she heard the dog call once only: it came from the Yat. Mary waved through the mist when she heard the dog again. A moment later Nan heard it; and she knew there was only one dog, and that the dog was Hewlin.

'It's all right,' she said. 'It's only an echo from the Yat: not Belanter at all. That's Hewlin, and we might as well go back to him and take him home.'

'I hate you ever so very much,' said Mary. 'It *is* Belanter.'

Nan went down to her, and brought her a little way up the hill and made her face the Yat. 'Call him loudly,' she said.

Mary called: 'Belanter.'

Out of the mist came the answer: 'Belanter.'

'Is that my voice?' asked Mary. 'It was a fairy.'

'An echo is a kind of fairy,' said Nan, carefully saying what would please Mary. 'But you can't see it: it can only say what you said to it.'

'There's other kinds too,' said Mary.

'Yes,' said Nan. 'But we'd better go and tell Forrest we've found an echo fairy. And we can take Hewlin home.'

'His name's Adam,' said Mary. 'What colour is a thing you can't see?'

They walked down the hill, and Nan tried to answer the question. Hewlin howled in the cloud.

CHAPTER SIX

SIGN LANGUAGE

Hewlin was sitting in the long grass watching three rabbit holes; he howled into them, and listened and waited, and howled again.

'Come on, you no-good,' said Nan. 'Time you went home.'

'All the rabbits have gone off and away,' said Mary, loudly so that the rabbits could hear.

Hewlin humped himself on to his four wet feet when Nan hauled on his collar. 'Take us home,' said Nan. 'Home.'

Hewlin sniffed at the ground, and started back towards Yowncorn Yat. Nan tugged him back. 'To your home,' she said. 'Or have I got to pull you?'

Hewlin agreed to go home. Nan made her mackintosh belt into a lead. She and Mary went down the hillside on their heels, with Hewlin pulling and waiting patiently and pulling again. He led them out under the cloud, along the slope, and came out at the Dig halfway down, close up against the pleated white skirt of water. He went down to a still by-pool to drink. Nan had to go with him, among the mossed rocks and wet perpetual ferns. The noise of the falling water hid the noise of Hewlin's lapping; the tumbling water dragged cold air with it; cold drops sprayed Hewlin's back and Nan's hair.

Mary stood alone on the slope, looking at the landscape and wondering where Africa began. Nan brought Hewlin away from the water: he seemed to be drinking the whole

waterfall; what made him thirsty was pulling his throat tight against his collar.

Mary thought of something else. 'I expect that's the way in,' she said. 'At the top of the Dig.'

'I expect it isn't,' said Nan. 'You're not to go up there.'

At the road Nan let Hewlin go. He went home and lay down on the bench in front of the inn. Mary ran before Nan to find Adam: he was not in the front of the inn, nor in the stable.

'Gone home again,' said Mary. 'Or perhaps he did lose himself in the mist on the way, even if he didn't want to.'

They found him painting an upstairs window frame at the back of the house. The clouds were breaking now, and the light of the washed sun came into Nan's eyes.

'Hello,' said Adam. 'I've nearly finished. I'm just cleaning up the brush marks on the glass.'

'Did you hear our Hewlin?' asked Peter. 'He's got himself bangled again among the rabbits.'

'We brought him down,' said Nan.

'He was talking to himself,' said Mary. 'Or, really, there was a fairy telling him what he'd said.'

Adam looked down from the ladder. 'How?' he asked.

Nan was behind Mary. She put a finger to her lips. 'It's what we heard,' she said. 'An echo fairy, wasn't it?'

'Yes,' said Mary, certain that with Nan on her side Adam would believe.

'Echo was a nymph,' said Adam. 'And that's a sort of fairy.'

Mary said 'Nymph' five times, and stored it away with other names of things. 'It's like a minim,' she said. 'You can draw it, and hear it, but you can't see a real one.'

'Well, there's another window done,' said Adam. 'Let's go and see what the signboard has to say for itself.' He came down the ladder with the paint and the brushes.

'Where's our Hewlin at?' said Peter. 'I'll tell him about making noises.' He went to find Hewlin; not to thump him but to look for thorns in his feet and twigs on his coat.

Adam banged the lid on to the paint can, and wiped green paint off his hands.

'We thought it was Belanter at first,' said Mary. 'We could have brought him here.'

'But it was only an echo,' said Adam. 'A lot of things are echoes. Echoes are fairies, and fairies are echoes: that's why you never see them easily.'

Mary approved of that as an idea: Adam was pleased to see her nod her head and smile.

He went into the stable. Sunshine sent a spark of fire on to the brass ring on the signboard.

'I gave it a shine up,' said Peter. 'Happen you could leave it like that, Adam.'

'I could varnish it,' said Adam.

'You might do,' said Peter. 'It took some cleaning: it was so very dirty. But it's our Hewlin's name. Come by, Hewlin, out of those spider-webs, honey.' Hewlin put himself down among the black webs. 'Gummock,' said Peter.

'I'll take the signboard paint off first, though,' said Adam. 'We might get an idea from the old pictures underneath this one.'

'Aye,' said Peter. 'Off with the paint then. See if there's any more underneath.'

Adam tore a piece off the sandpaper. He began to rub the bottom left-hand corner of the signboard.

The top paint was light green. Under the sandpaper it grew clean and bright, and the sandpaper grew black and green; then the green paint wore thin, and another colour began to show through.

'Brown,' said Nan.

'Red,' said Adam, changing to another part of the sand-paper. 'Look.'

In the corner of the signboard there was a small bright red patch, and another on the sandpaper.

'That's hard work,' said Adam. He stretched cramp out of his fingers.

'No words?' said Mary.

'Not yet,' said Adam. 'But now I know it works I'll try a bit in the middle of the board.' He chose the shoulder of the unicorn, and rubbed again.

The yellow-white shoulder wore away; colour came through from below: not red this time, but a black line, and a gold streak, and a white streak.

'Freaked with jet,' said Adam. 'It might be part of a word,' he told Mary. 'Let's do some more.'

Half an hour later the picture could be partly under-stood. The gold was a golden collar, set with coloured stones: blue, red, white and green; the collar itself was round the neck of an animal.

'I don't know what kind of creature it is, just from look-ing at it,' said Adam. 'But it must be a unicorn. They didn't paint a whole animal: it's only the head and shoulder.'

'What sort of gold is it?' asked Nan.

'Real gold,' said Adam. 'Gold leaf. It's very thin, you know. You can see through it if you hold it up to the light; and if you touch it with your finger it vanishes away.'

Mary touched the gold collar. Nothing happened.

'That's been glued down,' said Adam. 'Stuck on.'

'Clear some more off,' said Nan. 'We've to go soon: we shall be in trouble if we don't.'

'I'm going back at about eight,' said Adam. 'It takes me about an hour to get home: I live the other side of Thornton.'

'Ten to eight,' said Peter. 'Time for one more piece. Let's see the beast's head.'

Adam guessed at where the unicorn's eye would be, and cleaned away another patch of paint. Underneath there was a brown eye with a black border.

'It keeps looking at me,' said Mary. She went behind Adam to be out of its sight.

'Eyes nearly always look at you,' said Adam.' If they do in a drawing it shows they're drawn right.'

'We've only one minute left,' said Nan.

'Let's show Mrs Dyson first what we've done,' said Mary.

'If you like,' said Adam. 'It's her sign.'

Mrs Dyson came out with an old jacket of Peter's that she was cutting up to make into a rug. 'You won't need to paint another one,' she said. 'That's as bright as new.'

'Oh, but it'll be worn away,' said Adam. 'Or it'll have some other innkeeper's name on it.'

'It'll be Dyson,' said Mrs Dyson. 'It's always been Dyson here. Can you make another gold collar, Adam?'

'I might be able to,' said Adam. 'My father would know somebody who could tell me how. Did the unicorn have a golden collar?'

'Gold will make it bright,' said Mrs Dyson. 'But I don't know whether the unicorn had a gold collar. I always thought you had to catch unicorns with a grass collar woven by maidens.'

'You do,' said Adam. 'The beast becomes docile and obedient, with a grass rope round its neck.'

'What's a maiden?' said Mary.

'A girl,' said Adam. 'You're a maiden.'

'And I can catch a unicorn with a grass rope,' said Mary. 'How do you weave?'

'Oh, your ideas,' said Mrs Dyson, ruffling Mary's hair. 'What are you after? A gold collar?'

'A unicorn,' said Mary. 'I would like to catch it.'

'We shall catch trouble if we don't go home,' said Nan. 'It's gone eight o'clock.'

'I shall be coming soon,' said Adam. 'Can't you wait?'

'Mary's got to go to bed,' said Nan. 'But I shall still be up when you come.'

They went as fast as they could up the Screw, and over the top of the pass. The cloud was raising itself from the hilltops: Nan and Mary walked under it; but Yowncorn Yat and Wassand Fell were still shrouded.

'What noise does a unicorn make?' said Mary.

'I don't know,' said Nan. 'It stamps its feet, I think, like sheep.'

'Listen,' said Mary. 'Unicorns.'

'Those are only sheep,' said Nan. 'I've just told you about them. Sheep or rabbits.'

'It was foxes,' said Mary. 'Or the sun setting: you know it goes under the ground and back again to Wassand Fell. Look: it's already beginning.'

What Mary saw was the red light of the falling sun reflected from the Yat into the clouds: all the white layers were red; and the walls began to cast shadows from the east instead of from the west.

CHAPTER SEVEN

UNDER THE YAT

Adam came over the hill half an hour after Nan and Mary. Nan bathed Mary, because Mother was ironing: washing day goes on, whatever the weather. There was a smell of scorched iron-cleaning cloth, and a red fire with two flat-irons heating at the bars. The water was very hot, and Mary came out of her bath quite pink. She went outside barefoot in her nighty, half to see Adam, and half to look at the toad in the house labelled 'FRAG'. The toad was not there. Mary washed her warm muddy feet in Lew Gill, and made Adam carry her indoors.

'I'm sorry she's so cheeky, please, Forrest,' said Nan.

'You ought to see what happens when I go to the Head-master's house for special work,' said Adam. 'Nobody can keep his children in order.'

'Not even you?'

'Not even me,' said Adam. 'He says it's good for us to learn that we weren't born great, and haven't achieved greatness, but have had it thrust upon us to save the masters work. Now, what shall we do with this wet mermaid?'

'Put it back in Lew Gill,' said Mother. 'Come here; you've dipped the hem of your nighty in the water.'

Mary stood on a chair, and Mother ironed the hem of the nighty dry. When Nan came down from pushing

Mary into bed Adam was at the kitchen table kneading the bread dough and putting it into the bread tins.

'I always do it at home,' he said.

'Knead it until it squeaks,' said Nan.

'Teach your grandmother,' said Adam. 'I always go on till my hands are clean. There, Mrs Owland: do you think that will do?'

'Let's see your hands,' said Nan, not feeling in the least that she was talking to the Head Boy. Adam showed her his floury hands, just as if he were another junior.

When the bread was in the tins, spiked all over the top with a skewer (Adam's invention) and covered with a cloth and put to rise again, Adam said he had to go.

'I'll ride along with you,' said Nan.

'Half an hour,' said Mother to Nan. Nan looked at her watch to mark the time properly.

Outdoors in the bottom of the valley there was dusk; a bat flew out of the tractor shed and went on wafting wings hunting across the water of the Gill. At the head of the valley Yowncorn Yat was clear of clouds, and the red of the setting sun tinged the cliff.

'Have we time to get up there?' said Adam.

'Can't go on bicycles,' said Nan. 'We should have to walk. We might see a fox, as well.'

'We shall see the sunset,' said Adam. 'And I've got the beginnings of a sort of an idea.'

They went out past the new fence round the hens. Some of the birds had not yet gone to bed; they were still out gathering peck by peck scraps and creatures invisible to anything else, and keeping one eye on the sky, to see whether they had time to get back to their house before the night came on.

'Fox-proof fence,' said Nan. 'When the sun's on it it looks like a piece of glass.'

They crossed the wall where Charley had rebuilt it: there were newly chipped edges in the fabric, and broken corners and rubble in the grass. There was another wall to cross; it wandered over the high enclosure, and vanished in mid-field. Charley used it for a ready-cut quarry.

'Be careful about jumping over walls,' said Nan. 'There's a mineshaft here somewhere, near a wall.'

'This is where the unicorn and the hounds ran, isn't it?' said Adam. 'Straight up from your house to the Yat.'

'They always say so,' said Nan. 'They must have done, if the story is true.'

'It's the only story we've got,' said Adam. 'Of course, I don't believe in magic or fairies, or anything like that: but if the story is about nothing else, and there's no other story, then I suppose the only way to investigate is to see what the magic was.'

'We could try other things,' said Nan.

'It's like a problem in Geometry,' said Adam. 'You know, they put them in the book each time you've learned something new—riders, they call them.'

'You have to guess it,' said Nan.

'No you don't,' said Adam. 'You have to work it out from what you know. All we know is that nobody helped him: Dyson, I mean. He did it single-handed, or with the help of the fairies.'

'Nobody helped Gertrude Owland very much either,' said Nan. 'Fancy leaving her with nobody to look after her but some dogs and a unicorn.'

They had come along into a corner now, where the derelict wall met the boundary of the fell.

'Don't jump without looking,' said Nan.

'Bless you for telling me, Nan,' said Adam. 'Look at this.'

Nan climbed up on the wall beside him. 'I've seen it once,' she said. 'But I didn't know where it was again.'

Beyond the wall, immediately ahead of them, there was no ground. In its place was the square mouth of a shaft, with a steep sloping lip, and a vertical fall into darkness. Far below there was water moving. Adam picked up a small stone and dropped it into the middle of the shaft. It fell silently whilst he counted five; then it hit rock, and went spinning and singing and whanged into water.

'I shouldn't like to go perpendicularly into that,' said Adam. 'Come on: let's get up to the Yat, or you'll be late home.'

'Yes,' said Nan. 'She'll know when half an hour has gone, because of putting the bread in.'

They went round the pit, across light turf with rock underneath. There was a sharp rise, then a gentle slope down, then a succession of hillocks; and there was the smooth face of the Yat.

'It's like a castle wall,' said Adam. 'All grey and smooth. I suppose all the soft bits have worn away.'

'Everybody thinks it's been built, when they first touch it,' said Nan. 'But it's always been like that.'

Adam was looking round to find the highest ground under the Yat, so that he could look into Vendale. The far side of either dale was fully visible, and so was the sunset; but under the face of the Yat there was a shallow valley: the sunlight shone overhead.

Adam found a hillock thirty feet in front of the Yat. It was the highest place under the cliff; but not high enough to be touched by the sun.

'Can you climb on my shoulders?' he said.

Nan took off her shoes. Adam knelt; Nan stood up on his shoulders; Adam raised himself inch by inch, and Nan's head went up into the sun.

'Can you see the inn?' said Adam.

'The chimneys, that's all,' said Nan.

'What about your own house?'

Nan turned her head slowly. 'I can see all of that, and my own shadow behind me on the Yat.'

'Good,' said Adam. He collapsed her on to the ground. She put on her shoes, and accidentally looked at her watch.

'About three minutes to get home in,' she said.

They had to run down the hill. The sheep in each field leapt away, even if they were nowhere near, stamped their feet, and called to their lambs with their mouths full.

Nan arrived home two minutes late, just as the bread went into the oven. Adam recovered his breath and took out his bicycle. Up on the deserted fell a fox barked: a small sound reproving a cub. Mary looked from her window, and, seeing Adam, said: 'Listen: foxes.'

But Daddy was there by the tractor, to send her back into bed. Mary drew the curtains again, and got into bed.

'Hello, Adam,' said Mr Owland. 'I hope you haven't spoiled my chance of that fox. He came round last night, and I think he'll be here tonight, unless he comes across your tracks on the hill.'

'I'm sorry,' said Adam.

'The fox will be sorrier,' said Mr Owland. 'Or perhaps I should be sorrier to shoot it. That's the only thing I have against hens: I have to shoot the foxes. I'm expecting them to come and look at my piece of new fence.'

'Do you stay out all night?' asked Adam.

'Until about one,' said Mr Owland. 'Day's work tomorrow, as usual. Look, I've got another gun—stay if you like: two's better than one. We've a spare bed for you afterwards.'

'I'd love to,' said Adam. 'But I can't tonight, because I've a lot to do when I get home: my own homework.'

'Comes a bit hard to do two lots in one night,' said Mr Owland. 'Anyway, I don't think, after all, that I shall see the brutes tonight; not after you've been up there. But what about tomorrow night? I've got Charley, down at the cottage, but he can't see anything at night. But if you'd like a sleepless night, you're welcome—in fact, in great demand.'

'I will,' said Adam. 'I'll be here.'

'Good,' said Mr Owland: he wanted someone to share the blame with: he hated to shoot a fox. 'Don't say anything to Mary. She has at present in her funny little head a passion for foxes.'

'I know,' said Adam. 'Foxes and fairies. The trouble is, in this silver dogs' collar business, that the only things we know about are magic things: the help the fairies gave, and the digging of the Dig to get to fairyland, and Dyson being drowned.'

'And a unicorn,' said Mr Owland. 'But I don't know anything more about it.'

'I'm sure there's a reasonable explanation,' said Adam. 'But we've got to look at it as if it were magic. Anyway, I must go now: it takes an hour to get home. And I'll come tomorrow night and see what I can do.'

'Right,' said Mr Owland. 'Good night.'

Adam rode off over the plank bridge. Mr Owland took his cartridges out of his pocket, made sure the blue barrels of the gun were empty, and went indoors.

An hour later the risen moon shone over Wassand Fell, and made phosphorescent the pools of clouds lying in the heathery hollows; it shone into the mineshaft and lit with cold light the cold water running below; it shone through the cracks of the stable door at the Unicorn Inn, and lit the old eye of the revealed unicorn; it lit the heady water of Dyson's Dig. Hewlin saw it and whined at it. He was too lazy to howl again: besides, he lay on Peter's bed, and Peter would beat him for idle noise.

Under the Yat a fox watched and ran in the shadows, searching with her eyes the fences of Lew Farm.

Adam Forrest came to his house by moonlight.

Thoradale slept. When the moon was high the fox left

the shadows of the Yat, and went all round Lew Farm, finding the smell of the hens, and new bread, and tractor fuel, and Mary's lavender-soapy bath water where it ran over the yard. The fox looked into the house labelled 'FRAG', crossed the plank bridge, and went down towards the road for rabbits.

CHAPTER EIGHT

FOXES IN THE GARTH

The next evening Adam came to Lew Farm when tea was finished. He met Charley at the plank bridge.

'That old gun,' said Charley. 'It throws off to t' right. Thou keep it well ower to t' left, unless t' beast is going off to t' right.'

'Thanks for telling me,' said Adam. 'Did it come round last night?'

'It were laiking in t' valley bottom,' said Charley. 'T' old vixen, it were. Happen tha'd ha' copped her last neet if tha'd stayed. Ah'd be at it mesen, but Ah can't see owt in t' dark.'

'That's hard luck,' said Adam.

'Keeps me off t' poaching,' said Charley.

Mary came out of the door to shake the tablecloth. She saw Adam and called him in.

'Say nowt to t' little un,' said Charley. 'T' lass takes on so about t' foxes—aye, and as much again ower t' dead hens, so there's not so very much gained either road.'

Charley went home, riding his bicycle slowly beside the beck.

'We're just finishing the washing up,' said Nan, when Adam came in with Mary.

'You can't help,' said Mary. 'You weren't here.'

'I made the bread,' said Adam.

72

'Did you?' said Mary. 'It was like ordinary bread.'

'You'll have some for supper,' said Nan. 'And for breakfast if you get up in time.'

'Why don't you stop with Mrs Dyson?' asked Mary. 'She's got plenty of room.'

Mother had to come through then and explain to Mary that it was not the politest way of behaving to ask guests why they weren't staying somewhere else. But Mary had forgotten what she had said, and was wondering whether to let Adam have the day's only brown egg for his breakfast; and whether he would mind eating it upside down with his name on the pointed end: Mary's own name was on the round end. She went out to the tractor shed, to see whether his name was written on his bicycle. A. Owland was written on Nan's; M. Owland on the tricycle: there was nothing on Adam's but 'Hercules'. Mary looked at the word carefully and decided it was 'aircooled', which was what Daddy called the little motor of the dairy generator: a useful motor used for everything, from pumping water from Lew Gill, to painting with a spray, and cutting up wood.

She had a better idea. She went to tell the hens to lay another brown egg by breakfast time. They looked at her, but she gave them nothing to eat. They walked this way and that, stretching their heads forward first, and stalking up to them whilst they held them still.

'Gummocks,' said Mary, and went indoors again.

'Glaw, glaw,' said the hens.

There was no need for coats today. The clouds had lifted up, and floated on the outside of the sky. 'Like streaks of fat in a slice of blue bacon,' said Nan.

'With one fried egg floating across the dish,' said Adam, pointing to the sun.

'You two little ones must be back by eight o'clock,' said Mother. 'Adam, will you come down before dark?'

'Certainly,' said Adam.

'Can't you go to bed as late as you like?' said Mary. 'I shall when I'm a Head Boy.'

'Head Girl,' said Adam. 'I think they go to bed quite early.'

'Girl, then,' said Mary. 'Not so very much different. Or if I was queen of the foxes I would get up during the night and bark.'

Peter Dyson was coming up the Screw with Hewlin.

'You're belantered,' he said. 'It's half past six and after, and our mum wants her signboard back.'

'I told her it would take a week,' said Adam.

'Aye,' said Peter. 'She never said owt. But I'm waiting to see the pictures.'

'We're on the way,' said Adam.

'Come by, Hewlin,' said Peter. 'Come on, honey. I've a bone for you: come by.'

Hewlin was used to having Peter use up spare energy on him. He finished his walk to the top of the Screw, and then ran down again, got to the inn first, and went to sleep on the bench, feeling sure that hurrying home saved him a lot of trouble.

Mrs Dyson was indoors, still cutting up old clothes for a rug. Peter went in for the stable key.

They all went into the stable, and met the sunshine on the eye of the unicorn.

'It is rather starey,' said Adam. 'We'll get some more of the paint off, and see how old it is.'

He began again with sandpaper above the jewelled collar, and went up towards the top of the creature's head. He uncovered a tangle of mane, all marked in black and brown on the white, with a faded red background show-ing through. Above the mane was an ear. After that came the forehead; then the horn.

He did not have to search for long to find enough about the second picture. In the left-hand corner he found the date 1872.

'Not old enough to be worth bothering about,' he said.

'If it had said 1287 that would have been nearer to what we want. I shall have to go right down to the wood somewhere, and see how many pictures there are. But first I must stretch my hands again, because they get cramped.'

'Come on,' said Peter. 'Let our Hewlin keep field, bring a bit of wood, and we'll laike at cricket.'

Cricket was Hewlin's favourite game: everybody shouted at him, and he could do as he liked. Adam played for five minutes, then left the others and went back to the signboard.

When the cricketers stopped playing Hewlin took the ball away to eat it and the others came into the stable.

'Ten to eight again,' said Nan. 'Have you found anything, Adam?'

'Another unicorn,' said Adam.

'Is that little yellow line a unicorn?' said Peter. 'Come by, Hewlin. He's eating all the air out of that ball. Leave loose of that, Hewlin.' Hewlin let the ball go; Peter put it in his pocket. 'Aren't you right through the board?' he said. 'Isn't that the back of t' other side?'

'Not yet,' said Adam. 'It's the third picture; and there might be another.'

Mrs Dyson came out with some gingerbread. 'Something to go home on,' she said. 'You're making patchwork of that old sign, Adam.'

'Three unicorns so far,' said Adam. 'But what they're doing I can't tell. They're no help.'

'The sign may not be so very old,' said Mrs Dyson. 'Well, Mary, have you made your grass rope yet?'

'Not yet,' said Mary. 'The grass is only inches long. I didn't know it grew as long as ropes.'

'Have you never seen anybody spinning yarn?' asked Mrs Dyson. Mary never had seen that. Mrs Dyson explained how long strings are made of hundreds of short ones twisted together.

'Not like pigtails,' said Nan. 'They're all long hair: ropes are all short stuff.'

Mary gathered grass on the way up the Screw. When they got to the top she let it fly in the evening wind and lost it all.

'Flown off like banners,' she said. She was thinking of ropes and flags and processions, with someone who had caught a unicorn leading it docile on a green rope; and the people shouting.

'What would the queen say?' said Mary.

'She'd say we must hurry home to bed,' said Nan.

'Don't you go off with Adam tonight,' said Mary. 'If you want to go looking for things I'll come with you. You know it isn't safe.'

'Yes, your majesty,' said Nan.

Half an hour later Mary was put into bed, and the curtains were drawn. But she hopped out at once and looked between the curtains at the blue hillside, until her eyes closed, and she had to get back into bed.

Adam came at dusk. Nan locked the hens up, and closed the gates, all as usual. Daddy brought down the two guns from their beam in the kitchen, and told Adam one of them always threw its shot to the right.

'Charley told me,' said Adam. 'All our rifles at school fire crooked; I know which is which now, but it was awkward at first.'

'You don't have to be so dead accurate with a shot-gun,' said Mr Owland. 'But you've got heavy shot here and it won't spread a great deal. You'll have a second chance, though, with the second barrel. Anyway, we'll have supper first, seeing that it's Nan's feeding time as well.'

After supper Nan went to bed. Adam and Mr Owland smoked a cigarette each. Mother washed up.

'I wish I didn't have to do it,' said Mr Owland. 'But the egg money comes to a lot in a year. Take my advice, Adam, and go without daughters; they're expensive creatures. Then you won't have to feel hard-hearted about foxes. I had a fox cub when I was a boy; and it was a very pleasant creature if you didn't frighten it. But in those days birds weren't so important to the farm's economy. It's me or the foxes now.'

Darkness came up the dale. The little foxes stopped their romping to eat a small rabbit. The vixen left them, and lay in a dark place under the Yat, and watched Lew Farm.

'Moon up soon,' said Mr Owland. 'We'll go out now: we don't want to be out too long, and the sooner we're out the sooner she may come. Remember, it's your right barrel that shoots to the right: the other is straight.'

'Well, don't leave it all to me,' said Adam. 'I don't know how good I am with a shot-gun.'

They went out into the darkness: Mr Owland to the

tractor shed, and Adam to a corner of the farm garden, on the stone slab of the old larder. Each post overlooked the hen run and the field beside it.

They waited for the moon; the vixen waited for the moon.

CHAPTER NINE

A NIGHT WATCH

As silently as its shadow an owl flew over the farm garth; its wings seemed to be part of the air, and the shadow itself rippled over the stones, startling the mice.

Adam saw the shadow on the grass and as it climbed the white wire net. The vixen saw it from beyond the wall. There was no movement from the hen run: the fox turned to go. Then she came round again, through the sheep gate, and round to the back of the farm. Adam heard nothing and saw nothing. He stretched his fingers one at a time, and yawned, trying to stretch the beginnings of sleep out of his eyes. But though he dismissed it, again the music of sleep began sounding in his ears. The owl called: he heard it as a trumpet; a cockchafer whirred in the still air: he heard it as a drum; against his ear an ivy leaf moved under a spider: he heard in it the soft song of treble violins.

Then in a start he woke at once, still hearing music, but it was only Lew Gill lapping against the lonely water-stones. He was awake now, and the cold moon burnt coldly like frost on his hands and head.

Something stood in the field: black shape and black shadow. The vixen looked at the wire, and turned to go back the way she had come.

'I should shoot,' thought Adam. Though his hand

touched the gun, it did not want to pick it up and raise it in sudden movement. He watched the fox as if she were on a stage. She walked over the grass like a dancer: each leg had its attendant pointing shadow; the Gill still made rippling music. The fox made her own ballet, pointing each silent foot, and reached the shadow of the wall.

Under the tractor shed the moonlight moved: a straight gleam pointed to the fox; the night burst round the moving moonlight: twice there was thunder in the air; the fells sent the double report back from bank to bank and scar to scar. Every creature that heard crouched low and fearful; but one crouched animal heard nothing: shot moves faster than sound, and the fox was dead before she fell.

Adam saw his gun standing beside him, and knew he had not fired. 'Good,' he said. 'Oh good,' because he had looked at the fox with joy: as if it were a favourite dog or any dear beautiful thing.

Mr Owland stood up. Adam stood up, and the cold air bit into all the warm folds of his skin. He and Mr Owland stood over the fox.

'Did you do it, or did I?' said Mr Owland.

'You did,' said Adam.

'Oh, drat,' said Mr Owland. 'Why should I?'

'I'm glad I didn't,' said Adam. They looked down at the animal lying on the shadow of the wall.

'A vixen,' said Mr Owland. 'I think she's finished feeding her cubs: they'll be eating meat now. I shall have to watch for them in the autumn: they won't go far from here until they're hungry.'

'I think I went to sleep,' said Adam.

'I wish I had,' said Mr Owland. 'We'd better bury her now. Don't touch: she'll be covered with fleas.'

He went back to the tractor shed to find two mattocks and a crowbar, and a length of cord to pull the dead vixen with: a fox has a very strong smell that hangs on you if you touch. Mr Owland came back with the clattering tools, hitched the string round the fox's hind leg, and dragged her behind him into the middle of the field.

They started to dig. Mrs Owland came out in her dressing-gown to see what was happening.

'Oh, did you get one?' she said. 'Who did it?'

'I did,' said Mr Owland. 'First shot, behind the ear, and the second in the same place. Has Mary anything to say?'

'She's gone in with Nan,' said Mrs Owland. 'They're having a fight: they'll settle down soon.'

'Tell her it was an ugly savage great grandmother fox,' said Mr Owland. 'One that would have died in the winter in any case.'

'She'll forget about it if she doesn't see it,' said Mrs Owland. 'I'll get you a pot of tea ready.'

'Good. Hang these stones. Where's the crowbar?'

Digging a fox's grave was a quicker job than making postholes: the shape could be anything, and the hole need not be so deep. The damp stones came up shining in the moonlight, and the hole went down velvet dark.

'Enough,' said Mr Owland. 'Let's put her in.' He dragged the fox in, and let her lie, then put the stones over her, and filled the hole.

'Altogether,' he said, 'a fox is a better animal than a hen. But no one can do anything about that. Hens lay eggs: foxes don't.'

Ten minutes later the field was empty. The moon looked down on a little mound of stone and soil. The little foxes in the fell waited and watched. But they were awake in vain.

In the morning Adam and Nan went before Mary was up.

'I shall go to sleep this afternoon for sure,' said Adam. 'I almost do any day, especially when they will try to teach us French. And I always do during cricket. I'm a disgrace to the school. I don't mind batting, but I hate fielding, and I can't bowl. If they were fair they'd send me down with the juniors.'

'You'll wake yourself riding to school,' said Mrs Owland.

'I will,' said Adam. 'I'd better be off.'

Nan followed him in a quarter of an hour. When she had gone Mary came down, and went to look round the yard. She found nothing but the heap of stones in the field. She went indoors again, satisfied that if Daddy had done it, then it was right, but if Adam had, then he might have shot the wrong animal.

'He gets all cross if I tell him about fairies,' she said.

'Never mind,' said Mother. 'He's forgotten, that's all.'

'I wouldn't,' said Mary. 'It's not so very hard to remember.'

In the evening Adam met Charley at the plank bridge.

'Ah'd 've had a go, just so at t' boss wouldn't be so very certain who'd done it,' said Charley. 'But he won't even wring t' neck on a boiling fowl; though at trap shooting he awlus puts up a couple o' clays, and hits both on 'em.'

'I was hardly awake,' said Adam. 'And I didn't want to shoot it, either.'

'Well, Ah don't know,' said Charley. 'If you lived in a foreign place, you'd have t' tigers under t' beds alive, the way you go on. Thou and Mester Owland's a proper pair. Nay, Ah don't know. Ah mun be off for me tea.' He rode across the plank, shaking his head slowly.

'I would have missed,' said Adam to Nan. 'That would have been worse, I suppose.'

Mary came to see what was being talked about.

'Peter heard you,' she said. 'He nearly fell out of bed, and Hewlin knocked over a chair and slept on his clothes and emptied his pockets. We had to brush him at school.'

'Like Mary's little lamb,' said Adam. 'Against the rule.'

'Not *me*,' said Mary. 'And we had to brush *him*, not Hewlin. Hewlin stays at home. It was Daddy who did it, wasn't it?'

'Yes,' said Adam. 'I forgot all about shooting.'

'Good,' said Mary. 'But it would have been all right if you had written on the bullets.'

'Written on them?' said Adam. 'Written what, and what for?'

'You couldn't have done it if you didn't know its name,' said Mary. 'I wonder how Daddy knew. Did it have a collar? Do the old ones have collars?'

'I don't understand you,' said Adam.

'I don't either,' said Nan. 'But she means, do old foxes have collars? And how did Daddy know its name?'

'If he knew it was coming, he probably knew its name as well,' said Adam.

'He didn't say what its name was,' said Mary. 'But Mother said he wrote its name on the bullets; so they would be sure of shooting it and not another one when he didn't mean to.'

'Oh, I see,' said Adam. 'I should think he did write its name on the bullets. But I didn't know the name, so I didn't write anything.'

'He would have to shoot it even if he didn't want to,' said Nan.

'I know,' said Mary. 'If he tells me its name I'll put it on its grave.' She ran indoors to find a piece of paper to have ready at tea time.

'She likes names,' said Nan. 'She always wants one on everything. It's a good thing she can't write so very much.'

'What about your writing?' said Adam. 'Have you any homework to do?'

'Two lots of learning,' said Nan. 'One that Mary will like, about an elf having a feast of papery butterflies and cuckoo spit and ants' eggs. And then Marston Moor and Prince Rupert.'

'I can't learn it for you,' said Adam. 'I'll go on and clean up the signboard, and see whether Mary can find magic words on it.'

He left his bicycle beside the tractor, and walked up the gable of the dale. Nan sat down in the sun to learn her Civil War.

At tea time Mary found from Daddy that the fox's name was Reynard. With help she wrote it down, and after tea put the paper on the grave. Then they went over the pass to the Unicorn Inn.

Adam had not yet started the signboard today. There were still three windows he had not done, and there was the stable door, and the bench. 'And the signboard bar as well,' he said. 'I think I'll do it black.'

'What about the sign itself,' said Mrs Dyson.

'All colours,' said Adam. 'Blue in the background, and

black on the frame, and that horn-shaped part in gold. Not gold leaf, but gold paint.'

'It'll look very bright,' said Mrs Dyson.

'You'll get a lot of customers,' said Nan.

'I shan't be long with it,' said Adam. 'I'll finish this window now; then we'll go on cleaning the signboard.'

He went up the ladder again to finish the frame he was doing. The window was at the back of the house, so there was no room for the others to play cricket; there was too much garden stuff growing. Mrs Dyson went back indoors to her rug making.

'There's no ball either,' said Peter, when they decided against cricket. 'Our Hewlin yockened it down in minced pieces. And he got some toffee too. Old fool, aren't you, my honey.'

'I'm just finishing,' said Adam.

'I'm off to find another ball,' said Peter. 'We can laike at cricket whilst you slipe off that paint.'

When Mrs Dyson saw Adam come down from the ladder she brought out some gingerbread for everybody. They stood in the sun with the smell of green paint and pinks and sweet william round them, and ate gingerbread. Hewlin looked up at Peter.

'You chow on what you've got inside already,' said Peter. 'You sackless gummock.'

CHAPTER TEN

THE HOLLOW HORN

Adam yawned. 'This is very tedious,' he said. 'Does anyone think it's worth while going on?'

'No,' said Nan. 'You paint a new picture.'

'I ought to go on,' said Adam.

'You can't keep awake,' said Peter. 'I can't either so very easily, after yon noise last night.'

'It echoed like thunder,' said Adam. 'But I expect you went to sleep again. Mr Owland and I had to bury the fox.'

'Reynard,' said Mary. 'Same as his paper says.'

'Painted tombstone,' said Nan. 'Can't you paint a painted tombstone as well as a unicorn, Adam? You know, like the somebody or other who stepped this way at the trump of Doom's tone, from his painted tombstone. The Pied Piper.'

'Do one for me,' said Peter. 'I shall need it if you go firing any more guns without saying. I can hear anything that happens at Lew Farm. I hear your tractor start sometimes on a fine day.'

'Frosty mornings, perhaps,' said Adam. 'Sound travels anywhere on a frosty morning. It might even come over the pass if the air was still.'

'I thought you were in the road outside,' said Peter.

'Then our Hewlin got the ball, and ate it; and a piece of toffee.'

Adam looked in his box of paint. 'If you've got a chunk of wood I'll soon do you a tombstone,' he said. 'But first I think I ought to put a coat of paint on the sign-board, so that I can start the picture tomorrow. So let's sandpaper all the loose paint off, and make it smooth.'

Everybody could help at that. Adam tore a sheet of sandpaper into four pieces, one each, and they started.

'Have you found the fourth unicorn?' said Adam. 'Yes, you have. That's the best of the lot: it looks like a dear gazelle gladding me with its soft black eye.'

The fourth unicorn was a lifelike animal, standing quietly in green grass with its soft black eye gazing into the distance.

'No collar to it,' said Peter. 'No grass rope.'

At the mention of grass ropes Mary dropped her sand-paper and went in to talk to Mrs Dyson.

'She feels bound to catch one herself,' said Peter.

'We shall have grass all over the house,' said Nan.

Adam sandpapered away all the words at the bottom of the sign. They said 'Unicorn Inn' four times: only the top one saying 'Free House' as well; and that was all: the wood was below the last inscription.

'This side will do,' said Adam. 'It doesn't matter about the colour: I'm going to put a coat of blue paint over it all in a minute.'

'What about the carved horn thing at the top?' said Nan. 'Blue paint as well?'

'Gold paint,' said Adam. 'Sandpaper it if you like. But it's a fiddling thing, and I'll do it later.'

Nan tried the horn, then left it alone. If it had been a smooth carving she might have persevered; but it was divided in three by metal loops that clasped the wood, went round the horn, and up to form the hinges the board hung from. The paint was slightly sticky: it was almost tarry, and it stuck to the sandpaper.

Mary came back with a wisp of grass made into a short plait.

'It isn't hard,' she said. 'But you need a whole hayfield of grass, Mrs Dyson says. But you can all help.'

'We aren't maidens,' said Adam. 'Only you and Nan.'

'I'll wait until the grass is longer,' said Mary. 'It won't be so very difficult then.'

Adam blew paint dust out of the corners of the sign. He ran his fingers over the surface. His fingertips grew little rims of colour, and gold sparkled on the whorls of his fingerprints. He picked the sign up and turned it over.

'It's creaking,' said Mary.

'It's warped itself through lying on its side,' said Adam. 'That's nothing.'

Mary examined the name of Belanter engraved on the brass ring.

'What's the unicorn's name?' she said. 'If I write its name on my grass rope is that the same as writing it on bullets?'

'You don't know the name,' said Nan. 'Nor does anybody at all.'

'Our mum doesn't,' said Peter. 'Or she'd have told me; if she doesn't know it, who does?'

'You can catch it without knowing the name,' said Adam.

'Best thing to know it,' said Mary. 'But we knew Belanter, didn't we, and it was still only Hewlin.'

'He just didn't come,' said Nan. '*You* don't always come when you're called.'

'Nor does our Hewlin,' said Peter. 'Do you, honey?'

Hewlin was walking out of the stable, going slowly and carefully, and hiccupping.

'Off with you,' said Peter. 'It's that ball he's eaten: it's poisoned him, like.'

'He wants a piece of unicorn's horn,' said Adam. 'That'll cure him from any poison.'

'Will it?' said Mary. 'Hewlin won't die, will he?'

'He's off to leave loose of that ball,' said Peter. 'He won't hurt.'

'You might have to do two tombstones,' said Mary.

Hewlin crossed the road, and went to sit under the wall alone and quietly.

'The ball's still bouncing,' said Nan, going out to look at him.

'He'll want his supper when he's free of it,' said Peter. 'It's not the first time.'

'Well,' said Adam, thinking the conversation was too medical, 'what about your tombstone, Mary?'

'With a name on,' said Mary. 'And a fox, and a horn to blow up to call her with.'

'Why a horn? In case of poisoning?'

'Not a unicorn's horn,' said Mary. 'But like this one on the sign.'

'I could draw it on,' said Adam. 'Quite easy.'

'They may have used to blow this one,' said Mary. She was leaving moist fingerprints on the brass ring.

'Clean them off,' said Peter. 'I brightened that.'

'That's only a wooden horn,' said Adam.

'Don't wooden ones work?' said Mary.

'Blow it up and see,' said Nan. That was the quickest way of dealing with Mary: make her find out for herself what a thing was like.

But it was Adam who put down his sandpaper and looked at the small end of the horn.

'Don't encourage her,' said Nan.

'It's got a proper mouthpiece, like the one on the horn at Ripon,' said Adam. 'It might be a real one.'

'Go on,' said Mary. 'Try it.'

'Cautious investigation,' said Adam. He took his sandpaper again, and rubbed at the small end of the horn. Under the black paint there was red copper.

'This looks like something,' he said. 'It might be the hunting horn they used to call the hounds together with.' He rubbed again, halfway down the horn. He found the paint too sticky for the sand: it filled the paper and made it smooth and black.

'Tar,' said Adam. 'But more copper underneath.'

'Go on,' said Nan.

'Space for thought,' said Adam. 'That means the big

end is blocked up with wood. Gimlet, Peter—bradawl. A good strong one.'

Peter ran off at once to the cellar. Hewlin came in and lay down in the sunshine to watch. Adam was chipping off tar and paint with his penknife. Mrs Dyson came out with Peter to see what they had found.

'Eight o'clock,' said Nan. 'Hurry up.'

'I got a gimlet,' said Peter. 'Wind it in.'

Adam wound it into the wood in the bell of the horn. It went in, beyond the cut screw of the gimlet, and then slid forward into emptiness.

'Hollow,' said Adam. 'Can we break it off, Mrs Dyson?'

'Go on,' said Mrs Dyson.

'It's Mary being miraculous,' said Peter.

Adam shook the gimlet about, then pulled it out again. Peter thought of what to use next. He went in and came back with a chisel and a hammer.

Adam skived off a shaving of grey wood. Hewlin looked at the chip on the floor, and left it alone: the bounciness of the tennis ball was still in his mind. Adam tapped again; the chisel ate into the wood, and went through. It came out again, and there was a gap in the wood. Adam hooked two fingers into it and pulled. The wood sprang, and turned outwards; he tipped it back, and it came loose in his hand.

'You've bent the brass,' said Peter.

'Only a bit,' said Adam. He squeezed the bell back into shape, and dropped the wood on the floor.

He had opened the end of the hunting horn. The inside of the tube was visible.

'Anything inside?' said Mrs Dyson.

Adam tipped the whole signboard on to its edge, and shook it. There was a little gritty rattle of dust inside the horn. A pinch of dust fell out and floated away in the sunlight.

'Blow it up,' said Mary.

'I'm going to,' said Adam. He licked his lips, and bit them gently to make them soft. Then, still holding the sign on its edge he put his lips to the mouthpiece. It took him less than a second to find that the tube was blocked.

'White knitting needle: on the dresser,' said Mrs Dyson. Peter ran in to get it. Adam took it and pushed it into the small hole of the mouthpiece.

'The weather's got into it, I should think,' he said. He pushed again, then pulled the needle out. There was only half of it in his hand.

'The other needle,' said Mrs Dyson. 'Pull the sock off it, Peter.'

The second needle was the remedy. The broken half of the first one slithered out of the wide end of the horn; Adam pulled the whole needle out and gave it back to Mrs Dyson.

'Are you all ready?' he said.

'Hurry,' said Nan. 'We're supposed to be at home.'

Adam licked his lips again. He put them to the horn. There was a low, sweet, trembling note, filling the whole stable; as warm as sunlight; as strong as the brass metal itself.

Adam gave the note half a minute of life, and stopped to breathe in again the remembered echo.

'A long time since anybody heard that,' said Peter.

'Look at Hewlin,' said Mrs Dyson.

'Oh my honey,' said Peter. 'What's got you?'

Hewlin was standing up, every muscle drawn tense, each various yellow or black hair pricked into the air. He had raised his jaw, and he stood looking into cloudy distances: watching, listening.

'It's that ball,' said Peter. 'It's not all bounced up again yet.'

'I wonder,' said Adam. 'It's the sound he was listening to. But he couldn't. . . .'

'It called him,' said Mary. 'It's his name.'

'Where's Belanter?' said Nan. 'Is he . . .?'

'Nothing of the sort,' said Mrs Dyson at once. 'Adam, can you mend knitting needles? Now, Nan, Mary, off you go home. Peter, time you were going to bed.'

She sent them all out of the stable.

'I'll come over in a few minutes,' said Adam. 'Say it was my fault if you are late.'

'And no nonsense talk because a dog's got indigestion,' said Mrs Dyson. 'There's only one thing enchanted, and that's your wits.'

'Trump of Doom's tone,' said Nan to herself, recollecting the Pied Piper again.

CHAPTER ELEVEN

A GRASS ROPE

Mother looked at the kitchen clock. 'There's no need for me to say anything, is there?' she asked.

'Nine o'clock,' said Nan. 'Oh, honestly.'

'I don't know what that means,' said Mother. 'Up you go, quick, before I find you aren't in bed.'

'Supper,' said Mary.

'Not tonight,' said Mother.

'The horns of papery butterflies,' said Nan.

'A little fuzz-ball pudding,' said Mary.

'A strange diet,' said Mother.

'English homework,' said Nan.

'We have both learnt it,' said Mary. 'She can't forget it tomorrow.'

'You'd better have some milk whilst I'm not looking,' said Mother. She brought out the biscuit tin and opened it.

'We found something,' said Nan, when she had brought two cups of milk from the dairy. 'Didn't you hear it?'

'I heard nothing,' said Mother. 'Where were you?'

'At Mrs Dyson's,' said Nan. 'We found a hunting horn that they used to call the hounds with.'

'They'd certainly have one there,' said Mother. 'But I've never seen it.'

'Oh, you have,' said Nan. 'Every time you go.' She and Nan explained what Adam had found.

'I've never had so much dry biscuit spat at me before,' said Mother.

'You made us hurry,' said Mary.

'And did this hunting horn work?' said Mother.

'Easily,' said Nan. 'It wasn't hurt a bit.'

'It sounded like the last Amen,' said Mary.

'The trump of Doom's tone,' said Nan.

'The one in church,' said Mary. 'The one that won't let my legs keep still.'

'I know,' said Mother. 'All deep and shaking. It makes all the candles rattle as well.'

'Mrs Dyson said it was indigestion,' said Nan. 'But Hewlin thought he had to go hunting.'

'He wouldn't know anything about hunting,' said Mother. 'They haven't done any round here for years and years. It was given up long before Hewlin was born.'

'He ate the cricket tennis ball during the night,' said Mary. 'It bounced this evening.'

'You bounce to bed,' said Mother. 'Daddy will be in soon, and if he finds you you'll be slaughtered.'

Adam was next in, bringing a painted wooden tombstone for Mary.

'Put it in the porch beside the grass rope,' said Mrs Owland. 'Supper's in about half an hour.'

'I shall get some when I'm home,' said Adam. 'Thanks all the same, though.'

'I thought you were staying here,' said Mrs Owland. 'You might just as well.'

In the end Adam occupied the half hour before supper with going down to the school in Thoradale where the bus stopped, and ringing up his own home to tell them he would be staying away another night.

When Mr Owland heard about Hewlin's indigestion he was not so scornful as Mrs Dyson.

'Hewlin isn't much of a harrier,' he said. 'But he is descended from the hunting dogs, and they lived only for the chase; and the sign for the chase to begin is the sounding of a horn. I don't see why he shouldn't have a memory of what his ancestors did. Dogs do seem to remember things that never happened to them. You won't have noticed so much as I have, but nowadays even small puppies have more sense about motor cars than their great-grandparents had. It's a thing that rabbits never seem to learn; but dogs do know it: even dogs that have never seen a car.'

'How could they, scientifically,' said Adam.

'We shall have to invent a new science to describe it,' said Mr Owland.

'I should think so too,' said Mother. 'Any more tea, anybody? The next thing we know will be that someone has heard the hounds running under the fell.'

'Disbelief and heresy,' said Mr Owland. 'But I was only telling you an observation, not expecting a fable to come true.'

'Don't mention it to Mary,' said Mrs Owland. 'She's sure to hear it in the middle of the night, if you tell her.'

'I never met anybody who had heard them,' said Mr Owland.

That night the foxes were sadly quiet on the fell. The father of the little ones visited Lew Farm, and when he found what was there he sped away with no idea of hunting. On the fell again among the hungry family, he nipped their legs and sent them away from their home, and himself slept an hour or two. When the cubs came again still hungry looking for him he had gone: they never saw him again. They were alone.

Adam and Nan found Mary sitting beside a meadow making a grass rope. It was really a long plait: every time you brought the strand over you put in another stem of sweet balsam-scented grass; and the smooth head kept it in.

The plait of grass seemed to have one end floating in the air. Mary had tied one end to her own pigtail with her red ribbon to hold them both. The grass rope itself was nearly two feet long.

Mary left the meadow, bringing with her a handful of grass, to see what sort of homework had to be done today.

'No emmets' eggs this time,' said Nan. 'Plain ordinary arithmetic only; I did my Latin in the bus.'

Mary looked into the arithmetic; but she could make no sense of adding letters up: she did not know all the letters; and when it was all done even Nan could make no useful meaning out of it.

'It isn't hard,' said Nan. 'But it isn't interesting. It's not like adding up the eggs.'

'We have to add up minims,' said Mary. 'They aren't really there at all.'

Nan felt bound to do her arithmetic herself. Adam went with Mary to see whether the tombstone was dry. Mary had seen it, but left it alone, because the paint shone, and she thought it might still be wet.

'It's dry,' said Adam. 'Shall we put it up?'

Mary left the grass rope in the porch, and went with one unravelling plait to fetch a mattock. Adam dug up three stones, and propped the board up at the head of the grave.

'Her family might put flowers on it,' said Mary.

'They won't come near for a long time,' said Adam. 'Now I'll go to Mrs Dyson's, and finish off all the windows I've got to do. I expect I shall have finished when you come, and we can clean the hunting horn or paint a new unicorn for Mrs Dyson.'

'If we don't get back home late we'll be allowed to come,' said Mary.

'I'll bring you back myself,' said Adam. 'Just at eight. I'll go straight away, so that we can go straight on with whatever we do when you get there.'

Adam went over the pass. Mary went to Nan to have her pigtails tied together in the same ribbon, to save loosening the grass rope. They waited for tea.

The Unicorn Inn was full of the smell of fresh paint. Mary said she could smell it from the top of the Screw. Nan thought it was the fresh flowers of heather they smelt: the fells were starting to show their purple imperial cloaks.

Adam was right. He put the lid on the green paint just as Mary, running ahead, came to the inn door.

'What did I tell you?' he said.

'You should have told our Hewlin,' said Peter. 'Look at him leaned up against yon stable door.'

'Adam's got green paint on his ears,' said Mary. 'But not so much as Hewlin has on his side.'

'Adam's not sleeping on my bed,' said Peter.

'Is he all right?' said Nan. 'Hewlin, I mean.'

'Cobby as owt,' said Peter. 'But as soft as they come, leaning up against the paint like that. Come by, Hewlin.'

'Be careful how you go in,' said Adam. He pushed Hewlin out of the way and opened the stable door. Hewlin came in, breathing into the dust and raising it into the sunbeams.

The signboard lay on its trestles. It was painted

grey-blue, except for the horn itself, which was still black.

'We can take the horn off,' said Adam, 'and make the sign into an ordinary square one. The horn will be an interesting thing to have in the house.'

'It's fast on,' said Peter. 'How will you manage?'

'By bending the clamps that hold it,' said Adam. 'They aren't iron. I scratched them, and they're brass.'

He made the others hold the board whilst he tried to twist the clamps. But he accomplished nothing and gave it up. His hands came away covered with chips of tarry paint.

'It just moved,' he said.

'Hacksaw,' said Nan. 'It's what a plumber uses.'

In the end a hacksaw was not necessary. Adam found screws in the brass, holding the clamps to the wood, and when he had undone them the clamps dropped away and he slid the horn out of them. It was black in three sections, with three patches of metal: two dirty and one bright.

'It weighs nowt,' said Peter.

' Blow it up again,' said Mary. 'It wobbles me.'

Adam wanted to scrape away the sticky tar. He started to do it with his knife, and all the particles skipped from the knife into his eyes and mouth, and into everybody elses' eyes and mouth and hair.

'Now, stop,' said Mary.

'Stand farther away,' said Adam. 'You can, at least; but I can't.'

'Put it under water,' said Nan, remembering that she had had the same trouble with a burnt drip tin until she wet it and made the black particles heavy.

'Sowe it in the Dig,' said Peter. 'We'll get our Hewlin in as well.'

'It wants a wash,' said Adam. 'And if we get it under a waterfall we'll clean the inside as well as the outside.'

The lowest waterfall came out in a bow from the hillside. There was room to walk behind it in wet spray. The water went drumming down into a pool, and then flowed away in a quiet beck through a field and under the road. Beside and behind the fall everything was rush and noise.

Adam held the horn in water and scraped. The scraps of paint were snatched away as soon as they sparked off, and the metal with its smooth dull tarnish was left clear.

With the water to help him the whole operation took twenty minutes: the tarry paint was old, and did not hold readily to the brass.

'We must polish it,' said Adam. Nobody heard. Peter was there, but Nan and Mary had not wanted to get wet or be deafened: they had gone into the field seeking balsam grass.

The last flakes of paint scaled off. Adam let the water wash the curves of the horn. Then he stepped away from the fall and drained the water on to the grass. He put the horn to his lips and blew the second long blast. It was a shorter note than yesterday's: he had less breath today. The sound rolled out over Vendale, and returned to his ears, and stayed, and sounded again, and died far away under the sun.

'Our Hewlin again,' said Peter.

Hewlin was again watching the far distance.

'Trying to remember something,' said Adam, 'All his ancestors heard this sound.'

'They did that,' said Peter. 'Our Hewlin's one of them.'

'It must remind him of something he knows,' said Adam. 'He can't remember something he's never heard. I wouldn't believe it, whatever anyone said.'

'Put him in the Dig and let him forget,' said Peter.

'Yes,' said Adam. 'Or we'll start Mary off on some idea or other.'

'You let her be,' said Peter. 'She's very fendable on her own.' He meant she could manage things independently.

Nan and Mary came up with their grass.

'You could hear it for miles,' said Nan. 'All across the valley.'

'It's brighter now we've sowled it off a bit,' said Peter.

'But it isn't any particular use,' said Adam. 'Though I don't see why it should have a name on it if it wasn't for the hounds; and I don't know why they should put it up on the sign.'

'It's interesting,' said Nan.

'Come and do some painting,' said Mary. 'Nothing happens when you blow it.'

'There's our mum with spice cake,' said Peter. 'Come by, Hewlin. You won't get your washing today.'

CHAPTER TWELVE

THE SECOND SOUND

'I think time goes quicker over here,' said Adam. 'But it doesn't matter, because we get the gingerbread all the sooner.'

'We shall be slaughtered if we're late,' said Mary. 'I don't like being slaughtered.'

'You should have blamed Adam,' said Mrs Dyson.

'We'd better go early, all the same,' said Nan.

They had left the noise of Dyson's Dig, and they were watching the water from the inn. Adam had the hunting horn in his hand. Water still dripped from it. Hewlin looked at it every now and then, as if it were something he ought to know but had forgotten.

'Let me blow it up,' said Mary.

'Go on,' said Adam. 'Don't swallow it: it doesn't need to go into your mouth: just put your lips to it.'

'Don't spit it full of gingerbread,' said Nan.

In spite of Mary's deepest breaths no sound came from the horn except grunts of hard breathing.

'Your eyes will be out in a minute,' said Mrs Dyson. 'Or maybe you'll puff your tongue out.'

'You've made it as sticky as can be,' said Nan. 'I don't think I'll try it.'

'I'm going to brighten it tonight,' said Peter.

'You aren't, my lad,' said Mrs Dyson. 'You're to go off to bed, as soon as these go.'

'I can't do anything else,' said Adam. 'Not till I've made a square top for the sign.'

'There's our bench to paint,' said Peter. 'But I'll lock up our Hewlin while it gets dry.'

Mrs Dyson took the gingerbread plate indoors. 'See them off, Peter, and in you come,' she said.

Adam put away the paint he had been using in the stable, locked the door, and gave Peter the key.

'What about yon horn?' said Peter. 'I'll take it in, and happen get a go at brightening it. I'll put it under my bed, and say nowt to our mum.'

That was all the seeing-off he gave them; he went indoors at once with the horn, and took it upstairs quietly.

'I could have brought it with me and polished it for certain,' said Adam.

'He wouldn't let you,' said Nan. 'It's theirs, I suppose.'

'It is,' said Adam. 'I was thinking that it belonged to the story: but I don't think it does really. If it does belong what use is it? We don't know anything from it.'

'We learnt one new thing,' said Nan. 'The name of the other dog. We might find something else from it.'

Mary wandered all over the intakes, gathering red cock-roses, and letting the silk petals fall when she ran with the flowers in her hands. The broken stalks left sticky black marks on her palms. Nan was made to carry the balsam grass; and Adam the limp poppies. Then Mary imagined the other two held banners making procession for her;

and she walked along quietly, though the only crowds were sheep calling with their flat angry voices, and eating with their sideways-moving jaws.

'Listen,' she said. 'Foxes.'

This time she was right. There was a noise under the Yat; a sudden squabble, and after it quiet, and then one yelping bark. 'The little foxes are hungry,' said Mary, remembering the words of the black redskin she had met. 'But we don't know their names.'

'And a very good thing too,' said Nan.

They were saved from a quarrel by Adam, who threw a stone at something that moved. It was the cat; so they chased it home and into the kitchen, where it sat in front of the fire pretending it had never been out. Adam gave Mary her cockroses, bruised and wind-torn. He had left a trail of white-throated scarlet petals all the way down the hill.

'You've made better time today,' said Mother.

'Didn't you hear the horn being blown?' said Nan.

'Not a sound,' said Mother. Nan went out to ask Daddy. He had been in the yard all the evening, but he had heard nothing.

'Sounds won't come over the hill,' he said.

'Peter hears our tractor,' said Nan.

'He's mistaken,' said Daddy. 'There's plenty of other tractors he could have heard. But ours is in quite the wrong place.'

'It's a very loud horn,' said Nan.

'All the same, I didn't hear it,' said Daddy. 'What did Hewlin think about it?'

'He didn't say in words, exactly,' said Nan. 'He just looked the same as he did yesterday.'

'As if he'd swallowed a cannon ball or a chain-harrow?' said Daddy. 'I must watch him one day. It's what's called race-memory, or group consciousness: he remembers things that happened to some other dog.'

'Forrest said it was indigestion,' said Nan.

'They don't teach them science these days,' said Daddy. 'I may be quite wrong, but I don't want to be told so until I've proved I'm right; and I don't see how I could possibly do that until I can speak dog-language; and as I don't believe dogs have a language, I'm back where I started.'

Supper time came; and supper. Bed time came to each in turn. Midnight passed; one o'clock, and two o'clock. Nan woke just before two, and read the luminous dial of her alarm clock. In the next room Mary was lying on her back and snoring. She would wake up in a moment and turn over: Nan often woke up to hear her do it: sometimes it was best to go and turn her if she didn't wake herself up. In the meantime Nan looked at her own room in the quiet moonlight. She drew back the curtains a little more, and let a wide band of moonlight in. The open window showed the fells and Yowncorn Yat dressed in silver, like the mountains of the moon themselves.

All the light was silent. Nan looked at it, and thought about the world that Mary was always on the edge of finding.

Out of the silver picture came a silver sound: the long note of a horn sounded clear from the south-east, from the tall bright cliff of the Yat. One note died in the night: another followed. Mary stirred and started in her bed. Her feet thumped on the landing, and she was at once clinging

to Nan in the moonlight, all warm and blinking with sleep.

'They've come back,' she said. 'The hounds.'

'That's all right,' said Nan. 'We're a dream. Go to sleep, darling.'

'Not a dream,' said Mary. 'I can taste it isn't. We must go out and tell them.'

'There it is again,' said Nan. The horn sounded a third time, high and clear. In the next room Adam sat up.

'Tell him,' said Mary. 'Now he'll know.' She leaned up at the window, listening and watching.

Nan found Adam doing the same thing. But outside there was no sound.

'That wasn't our horn,' said Adam. 'Ours is a low note.'

'It's a golden one,' said Mary, from the next window. 'Let's go and see.'

'In the morning,' said Adam. 'Not now.' He found nothing to make sense of or think about: the only explanation in his mind was Mary's: that the hounds had come back and were running under the fell; and no part of his mind would believe that.

'Now,' said Mary. Stirring a sudden transport she started to cry, not fearfully, but as if something had been taken from her. Nan went back to her. She was lying down, weeping on to Nan's pillow, and a minute later she was asleep. Nan covered her up.

'We imagined it,' said Adam, the last clingings of sleep falling from him. 'Go back to bed, Nan. It was the long moonlight in our eyes, making us dream.'

'Three people dream the same dream,' said Nan.

Another door opened. 'What's all this palaver,' said Mother.

'We heard a noise,' said Nan. 'But it's stopped now.'

'I should think so too,' said Mother. 'Who's this in your bed?'

'Well, it's Mary, of course,' said Nan. 'She woke up and came through and went to sleep again.'

Mother picked Mary up, kissed her, and put her in her own bed. She came back and drew Nan's curtains, and everybody went to sleep again.

Getting up in the morning Nan thought the sound of the night was a dream. The memory seemed to be mounted in sleep: a single lantern in a dark world, bright and evasive.

'How many times was it?' said Adam.

'Three,' said Nan.

'It was us,' said Adam. 'I think anything at night.'

During breakfast, before Mary was down, Mother asked them what it was that woke them.

'A horn or bugle,' said Adam. 'Only one note, and that sounded three times.'

'At five to two,' said Nan.

'And it wasn't the horn I found at the inn,' said Adam. 'The notes were quite different. Besides, who would blow it at five to two?'

'A fox howling,' said Mr Owland. 'Or a lost dog.'

'Nothing of the sort,' said Adam. 'We heard a bugle because we were expecting to; but it was some other sound really: we weren't properly awake: our senses misled us.'

'My fault for talking about Hewlin remembering things that didn't happen to him,' said Mr Owland. 'There's dozens of things it might have been: rock sliding in some scar; or wind eddying in a chimney.'

'No wind,' said Nan.

'Or a bird with a sore throat,' said Daddy. 'But *not* a pack of magic hounds.'

'Mary said . . .' said Nan.

'Of course she did,' said Daddy. 'She's practically a

savage: all little children are. She doesn't know yet which things are real and which are unreal.'

'All stories are true to her,' said Nan. 'I know.'

'And in the end you aren't brought any nearer to finding the lost dogs,' said Daddy. 'You'll just have to look on the fell: and you won't find anything.'

'We shall,' said Adam. 'We haven't looked anywhere yet; and see what we've already found.'

'A name that might be a dog's,' said Daddy. 'And a retired hunting horn and a moth-eaten legend.'

'Nothing that belongs to anything,' said Adam. 'All separate things, really. All the same . . .'

'You might be lucky again,' said Daddy.

Charley waited for Adam at the plank bridge in the afternoon.

'What's this our little Mary says?' he asked.

Adam told him what they had heard in the night, and what the explanation might be.

'Nay,' said Charley. 'Birds nowt. You've called them hounds back, tha knows. They'll be running again to-night. Nay, but Ah'd like to coome up and hear 'em. Happen it's never none but t' Owlands as ever did. It's a right queer do.'

'No bad luck, or anything?' said Adam.

'Nowt Ah've ever heerd on,' said Charley. 'But it's not heerd of at all so very often.'

'You can listen,' said Adam. 'But can't you hear it from your house?'

'Nay,' said Charley. 'Nobbut from Lew Farm. It's t'
only place.'

'Curiouser and curiouser,' said Adam.

Mary had her plait of grass rope round her waist, and a
pile of grass beside her in the porch.

'I'm going to take it to bed,' she said. 'The unicorn's
with the hounds. And I shall catch it.'

'Then what?' said Adam.

'Me and Peter will ride it,' said Mary. 'He says he won't,
but I'll make him.'

'Did he hear anything?' said Nan.

'I think he did,' said Mary. 'He said he didn't, but then
he said he was awake, so he must have heard it.'

'Four people dreaming,' said Nan.

'What about Hewlin?' said Adam.

'He had to sleep in the woodshed,' said Mary. 'Peter
wouldn't say anything at all. I think Mrs Dyson was cross
for something. He wouldn't even pull my tricycle up the
hill. So I sent him home alone.'

'H'm,' said Adam. 'I wonder. And Charley says no one
ever heard it except from Lew Farm. However, doh, me,
soh, doh.'

CHAPTER THIRTEEN

BATS WITH A BRUSH

Peter went away when Adam came to the Unicorn Inn. He hid in the garden, and pulled up the tiny groundsel beside the briars. Mrs Dyson was out: the stable door was open, and her bicycle gone from inside. Adam thought Peter must have gone with her. Hewlin was there to keep house: but Adam saw nobody else.

He began to shape the top of the signboard. Luckily the frame was of the plainest possible sort, and very easily matched. Before Nan and Mary came down from Thoradale he had finished squaring the sign and was painting the bench outside the inn. He dragged it from its place, and put one end on the garden wall to make it easier to get at and worse for Hewlin to lie on and decorate himself. Peter had left the shelter of the raspberries, and sat under the garden wall, all among the dust Adam brushed from the two legs of the bench overhanging him: but Peter was there first and had no opportunity to crawl away. He watched Adam's hand moving all alone, working green paint into the corners of the bench.

From the top of the Screw Mary saw Peter lurking in his hiding place. When she got down she hauled him out. He came sulkily and stood beside Hewlin.

'Don't be so rough with him, Mary,' said Adam.

'He was hiding from you,' said Mary.

'Perhaps he was just creeping up,' said Adam. But he had seen many juniors with misdeeds burdening their minds. Peter looked like one of them now: he had done something he was half ashamed and half proud of. And that was a thing that always made juniors troublesome. But Adam had guessed what the sound in the night was. Here was Peter, wanting to say he had blown the horn during the night— blown it better than Adam—and afraid that Adam would be extremely angry. As well as that, Peter had some idea that if Adam disapproved of him, then, even if he passed the exam the Grammar School would not have him.

Adam was not in school now. 'How did you manage to find the octave on the dominant?' he said.

Peter had no idea of the meaning of octave or dominant; he knew they had to do with the horn; and there was no scorn or reproof in Adam's voice.

'Eh, Hewlin, shift over,' said Peter.

'It's all right,' said Adam. 'I know it was you.'

'But it was quite a different note,' said Nan.

'Doh, me, soh, doh,' said Adam. 'I found out from our bugler today. You can sound quite a lot of notes from one horn by squeezing your lips.'

'Press harder,' said Peter. 'It makes a noise and all, if you heard it over there.'

'All the notes have different names,' said Adam.

'Minims,' said Mary. 'You played minims, Peter.'

'Perhaps they were,' said Adam. 'I don't know. But our

bugler says it was an octave on the dominant. Don't ask me what it means, because I don't know.'

'I do,' said Peter. 'It meant our mum came in and gave me bats with a brush.'

'It must have been a shocking noise for the middle of the night,' said Adam.

'You won't tell them at the Grammar?' said Peter.

'No,' said Adam. 'What should I do that for?'

'Our mum thought you might,' said Peter.

Mrs Dyson rode up on her silent bicycle then, and heard Peter. 'Our mum thought nothing of the sort,' she said. 'Our mum just thought there was enough nonsense going on, that's all: and if there was any more our mum would have a strong word to say all round: Adam Forrest as well.'

'I'm sorry,' said Adam.

'It's all right,' said Mrs Dyson. 'But you didn't hear that thing during the night. If you had you'd tell them at Thornton all right. I thought it was a cow on the roof.'

'She did and all,' said Peter.

'Until I laid hold of that hairbrush,' said Mrs Dyson.

Adam explained how the sound had been heard at Lew Farm.

'I wish it wasn't only Peter,' said Mary.

'Nobody heard it in Wassand,' said Mrs Dyson. 'I'm glad to say. But it shows how stories start. Look what it made you think, when you were half asleep.'

'It's nothing to what you thought,' said Adam. 'A cow on the roof.'

'All forgiven and forgotten,' said Mrs Dyson. 'But don't do it again.'

Adam had not stopped painting. When Mrs Dyson went indoors he finished the last stroke. 'I can't see anything else unpainted anywhere,' he said. 'Shall we go and design a unicorn? Then I can spend all day at it tomorrow.'

'Play cricket,' said Mary. 'Or go for a walk.'

Adam suggested stirring paint, and that seemed more interesting than cricket. They took Hewlin into the stable and put him in a corner.

'I can brush off the mus-webs,' said Peter. 'But the old fool's fond enough to climb on to the bench, and I like him to sleep on my bed better than in the fire-kindling in the shed. He bites up all the twigs, and they won't burn.'

Adam's idea was a plump prancing unicorn walking on a green field, with the sun above to throw shadows.

'Put in the Yat and the Dig,' said Nan.

'And me leading it with a grass rope,' said Mary. 'And put in the two dogs.'

'Come by, Hewlin honey, and get your picture made.'

'Two yellow dogs? Why not?' said Adam. 'And a hunting horn. And a Yat and a Dig.'

'Not forgetting the unicorn,' said Nan.

'I'm not making the Bayeaux tapestry,' said Adam. 'It's the unicorn first, and the other things round the edges.'

Before they had decided what to do Peter put both hands on the newly painted top of the board.

'You and Hewlin between you . . .' said Adam. 'Do you lick it off for the taste or something?'

'I'm tattooed,' said Peter. 'Like a sailor. It's not so very sticky either.' He went into the garden to work the paint off in the soil. He accidentally found another ball, so they

played cricket in the road with three bean-poles in Adam's first empty paintpot for a wicket.

'I can't do any painting tonight,' said Adam. He bowled, and got everybody out in three shots, and broke two of the bean-poles again, so that they continued with five assorted stumps instead of three the same length.

Nan tried to bowl him out, but all her balls bounced over his head.

'You can't go in just because you've merely killed the batsman,' said Adam. 'Look, don't think about the wicket; think about getting the ball to a place where it'll bounce up behind the batsman. It bounces off at the same angle as it hits the road: if you throw it low it'll stay low, and it'll be going upwards from the bounce when it hits the wicket.'

'They can do it without all that bookwork,' said Peter.

'It's useful to know,' said Nan. 'It would be better if he wasn't there to hit it, though.'

'Nothing like a bit of science,' said Adam.

Nan at that moment sent a ball that went nowhere near the ground: it knocked over the remaining long stump by touching the top. The stump fell down and broke; the ball trundled off into the grass.

'OUT,' said Peter in his loudest voice.

'Don't,' said Mary. 'Mother would hear that.'

'You don't need a trumpet,' said Nan. 'Horn, I mean.'

'Here, wait a minute,' said Adam. 'Peter, where were you when you blew the horn?'

'In bed,' said Peter. 'Under the happings, with the end of the horn out of the window. That one up there.'

'But we heard it from the fells,' said Nan. 'Didn't we, Adam?'

'Yes,' said Adam. 'It's just what I was telling you about the bouncing ball. Noises bounce just the same. Did you hear Peter's voice echo all over just now? Well, so would the horn.'

'Off the fells?' said Nan.

'Off Yowncorn Yat,' said Adam. 'Now, wouldn't it, if he pointed it to the Yat? It would echo off the Yat: the sound would bounce off.'

'It would go anywhere after that,' said Peter.

'It would bounce off at the same angle,' said Adam.

Peter had no way of knowing what Adam meant.

'Can you pat a ball?' said Adam. 'You know, so that it jumps up into your hand again.'

Nobody could but Mary. Adam gave her the ball, and made her pat it. 'Look, if it goes down quite straight then it comes up quite straight: if it goes down slanting it comes up slanting, but farther away.'

The explanation was still not clear to Peter.

'Book work,' he said. 'They bounce without words.'

'It's geometry,' said Nan. '*I* know it.'

'Even if you don't know it,' said Adam, 'we've found out how the magic was done.'

Mary let the ball run away and came to hear what Adam had to say.

'Dyson didn't have to go to the fairies,' he said.

Mary looked at him with the look schoolmasters use when you tell them carefully that four fives are thirty-six.

'I know you don't believe me,' said Adam. 'But I don't believe in fairies, so I've got to believe something else.'

'You haven't,' said Mary. 'Mother says it doesn't matter what you say, because you've forgotten.'

'When Dyson blew the horn here the sound went up to the Yat, echoed off it, and went down to Lew Farm,' said Adam. 'Remember, Nan, we went up there, and you can see the farm and the inn quite clearly, with nothing in the way. The hounds heard the horn, and went off to the Yat, and Dyson went up the Screw, let Gertrude out, and got back here while the hounds were at the Yat, looking for someone who wasn't there.'

'All bangled, like our Hewlin,' said Peter.

'Probably,' said Adam. 'You see, it would be too dangerous for Dyson to go up anywhere near the dogs. He would have to call them so that they went a long way round—so that he could get to Lew Farm first.'

'It sounds quite clear,' said Nan. 'And what about the hounds hunting under the fell? How did Dyson arrange that?'

'All he had to do was blow the horn again,' said Adam. 'The sound would come from the Yat again. Everybody would think there was something up there. Dyson could tell them it was fairies to keep them away.'

'Silly,' said Mary. 'Of course they're there. You can't have two stories.'

'Not with both of them true,' said Adam. 'You can if one of them's an old one gone wrong.'

'Stories are true,' said Mary.

'Not all of them,' said Adam. 'Really, you know, Mary, they aren't.'

'Well,' said Mary. 'How could the hounds get into fairyland unless the fairies let them in?'

'Oh,' said Adam. 'Oh. That's a difficult question. Why did only two hounds escape? And what did they escape from? What happened to the others? Where did they really go?'

CHAPTER FOURTEEN

AN OCTAVE ON THE DOMINANT

'See,' said Mary. 'Mother said you had forgotten.'

'I haven't forgotten,' said Adam. 'I never knew.'

'You can't know anything different from the story,' said Mary. 'If you did it wouldn't be true.'

Adam remembered how Nan turned conversations round so that Mary had to finish them by finding out for herself.

'I haven't seen the gate to fairyland,' he said. 'How can I tell whether it's true?'

'It's the Yat,' said Mary.

'Of course it is,' said Nan. 'Isn't it, Mary? It's either the Yat, or somewhere near it, but very hard to find.' Nan had made up some of that; but Mary took it to be true, because Nan was on her side, not Adam's. Nan was thinking mostly of how to stop Mary from being so rude to Forrest: Nan knew pretty well what Mary thought about fairies and magic; and she realized just as well what Adam thought of them. Adam's point of view was like hers, but she believed in the story not at all; and Adam thought it was true without magic. And, though Adam might not mind Mary saying anything she liked to him, he might think it was Nan's duty to stop her. Adam, Nan thought, was no good at arguing with Mary: if you put it the right way Mary would believe anything you told her.

'It's up there,' said Mary.

'You mean it's just on the hill?' said Adam.

'One side or the other,' said Nan. And then a way of satisfying Mary came to her mind; but at the moment there was no need to say anything.

'Well,' said Adam, just as Nan had hoped, and just as he had hoped. 'Find it for me, and I'll believe you.'

'I shan't ever believe you,' said Mary. 'Never never.'

'Come on,' said Peter. 'Don't be so yonderly. You should be batting, Nan.'

'I know,' said Nan. 'We're just talking about treasure.'

'I know *that*,' said Peter. 'But happen it's my treasure when you do find it, so you can give over talking about it, and laike at cricket.'

'You bowl, Peter,' said Adam. 'The ball's run down the road.'

They played cricket until the bean-poles were merely twigs. 'They'll do for fire-eldin,' said Peter. 'It's what they were for.' He gathered up the sticks and took them to the woodshed.

'For Hewlin to sleep on,' said Nan.

When Peter came back he brought a plate of gingerbread with him. 'This is something like,' he said.

'I'm thirsty,' said Mary. They went to the bottom of the Dig and drank falling water.

'We ought to boil it first,' said Adam. 'We don't know where it comes from.'

'It comes straight out of a hole in the earth,' said Nan. 'I've seen the place often. It comes rushing out and falls straight down here. There aren't any germs in it.'

'Happen not,' said Peter. 'But it's a drowner, isn't it, Hewlin?'

'No use asking him,' said Nan.

'It's where Dyson was drowned,' said Peter. 'There was a Hewlin then. They'll have told him.'

'I wish I could speak dog language,' said Adam. 'I should just ask Hewlin what they told him about the rest of the pack, and he would tell me what happened to the treasure.'

'Fairies,' said Mary.

Adam said nothing. Hewlin looked for gingerbread crumbs.

'We'd better go home,' said Nan. 'It doesn't matter really if we are late, but if we are we shan't be able to go up with the egg van tomorrow night.'

'In winter he comes at midnight,' said Mary. 'I'm always asleep.'

'In the dark, anyway,' said Nan.

'If you're going,' said Adam, 'tell Charley that if he comes to your house at ten o'clock there'll be something he's interested in.'

'I know,' said Nan.

'If I can manage the octave on the dominant,' said Adam. 'Perhaps I'd better practise first.'

'I could do it,' said Peter.

'You'll be in bed,' said Adam. 'I want to do it as late as I can, when the dew's fallen, because sound will travel better then.'

'Our mum wouldn't know if I did it,' said Peter.

'Something will happen to you,' said Mary. 'You shouldn't tease fairies.'

'Nothing will happen to us,' said Adam.

'Mrs Dyson will give you bats,' said Mary. 'That's not so very nice. That's one something.'

'That was our mum,' said Peter. 'Not fairies or boggarts or owt else.'

They walked back to the inn. Adam took the empty gingerbread plate in; and he came out with the horn.

'She doesn't mind,' he said. 'But I've to polish it so it can be hung in the bar.'

'Nay, well, I want to brighten that,' said Peter.

'You're welcome,' said Adam. 'Now, listen.'

'Squeeze your lips up,' said Peter. 'And it makes you that dizzy.'

Adam lifted the horn to his lips. His first note was the low thrilling tonic he had blown before. The second note made a queer skillocking jump in the middle; the third rose straight up, an interval of a twelfth: the high, sure, calling tone that had woken Lew Farm in the night.

'Done it,' said Adam. 'A whole octave.'

'Why don't they come back, then?' said Mary.

'May be a long way off,' said Adam. 'It might take them five years to come back.'

'Seven years,' said Mary. 'That's the time it should take: it's seven years after they've eaten anything.'

'If they're like our Hewlin they'll never be out,' said Peter. 'They'll have been yockening it down as fast as they can get. What if it's a tennis ball, and they cough it out again?'

'You can shut up,' said Nan.

'Yes, you can,' said Adam.

'Fairies can't play cricket,' said Mary. 'So you aren't arguing.'

'We've got to go home really,' said Nan. 'I'll tell Charley to listen, but I won't tell him why.'

'He knows,' said Adam. 'Come on, Peter. What about this polishing business?'

On the way home Mary was busy thinking about something else, not whether Adam was right or where the hounds were.

Nan was wondering quite how much help it was if Adam did sound the horn and show how it echoed off the Yat. It would prove what Dyson had done, perhaps, but it would only make Mary more sure of Fairyland, without helping Adam to provide any other explanation.

'What are you doing?' said Nan. 'Pretending to be a fairy?'

'Being an egg,' said Mary. 'First I'm laid, then you find me, and then I'm put in the box, and then somebody boils me and carries me to the table, in their hand, you know, and then they open the top and I say hello.'

Before they went indoors they went across the plank to give Adam's message to Charley.

'They learn them summat at the Grammar,' said Charley. 'Ah'll be up by ten, never fear. Is there owt to see? Ah'll none see it that late on.'

'Only a sound to hear,' said Nan.

'It's a right do,' said Charley. 'They used to say it was Owland money them dogs was carrying, and there wasn't an Owland could bear to hear it. But t' money isn't what it was: it's none so vallibel or worth so very much: Ah don't know what we'll do when it isn't worth nowt.'

'Gold and silver,' said Nan. 'We'll still have those.'

Daddy was repairing something on the side of the tractor. Nan told him what Adam was going to do.

'It's a pity there's an explanation, really,' said Daddy. 'But perhaps we have to have them. Music at ten, is there?'

'They might come back,' said Mary.

'I hope not,' said Daddy. 'Where are we going to keep them?'

'A unicorn instead of a tractor,' said Mary. 'They're tame, like cats.'

'It would be very unusual,' said Daddy. 'But I don't think there's any law against it; though there might be.'

Mother was darning and waiting for Mary to come in. 'I'm glad there's a sensible reason for it,' she said, sliding the long-tailed needle through one of Mary's brown heels. 'Though reasonable isn't what I should call Peter. The hairbrush is what he deserved.'

'Not really,' said Nan.

'Waking everybody up,' said Mother. 'I very nearly did the same to you three.'

'Adam too?' said Mary.

'Yes,' said Mother. 'Big stick for him. And now I suppose nobody will go to sleep until the horn has sounded. But you'd better go to bed, for all that.'

Mary in a dark room could not last until ten o'clock; she was asleep when the horn sounded from the throat of advancing night. Three times it called: the third time the note broke in the middle.

'Run out of breath,' said Nan.

'Pomposity of elfin orchestras,' said Daddy. 'Dying, dying, dying.'

'It's a queer thing to have made out,' said Charley. 'It's queer, isn't it, Mr Owland?'

'It explains what Dyson might have done,' said Mr Owland. 'But it says nothing about the Dig, and the way he was drowned. Now, if it would uncover the treasure for us, that would be something.'

Half an hour later Adam came over the pass.

'Did it work?' he asked.

Nan came down to the bottom of the stairs to hear what they had to say about it.

'Went off very well,' said Daddy. 'Except your last note: that cracked in the middle.'

'Peter jogged my elbow,' said Adam. 'You know, we thought we saw the hounds coming out of the hillside.'

'You mustn't,' said Mother. 'You'll have Mary talking of nothing else for the rest of her life. Haunted grandmother, she'll be.'

'It wasn't hounds,' said Adam. 'Only a pair of fox cubs having a scrap in full view of everybody, just up above the

Dig. They were very small, quarrelling over something even smaller—a beetle, perhaps.'

'So long as it's not my hens,' said Daddy. 'Or we should have another night up. But I'm glad in a way to hear they're still alive after the vixen has gone.'

'Quite lively,' said Adam.

'I hope they keep away,' said Daddy. 'Peter anything to say about them?'

'He tried to send Hewlin up, but Hewlin only got into the middle of the field, then he was bangled, whatever that means, and he had to be brought back.'

'The horn doesn't excite him now?'

'It does,' said Adam. 'Otherwise he wouldn't have gone up at all.'

'He has no wits,' said Mother. 'That's your tea in the blue cup.'

Nan crept up to bed again.

'Is it ten yet?' asked Mary.

'Gone long ago,' said Nan.

'Did you hear it?'

'Easily,' said Nan.

'Did the dogs come?'

'No,' said Nan. 'They saw some foxes instead.'

'Just as nice if they came,' said Mary. 'They wouldn't take up any room.'

CHAPTER FIFTEEN

A WET ROPE

Mary found and wrote three brown eggs before Nan came to the henhouses. Mary had only looked for brown eggs: Nan when she came had to chase the birds out again to gather the ordinary white eggs.

'I can't read your writing very well,' she told Mary. 'Is that an N or an H or an A?'

'D for Adam,' said Mary. 'It's your pencil.'

Nan pulled a chaff-laden cobweb out of her hair and collected the last eggs from the hen-warm straw.

'Egg washing,' said Mary. 'Before breakfast.'

'If you like,' said Nan. Mary went in to get a bowl of water and the egg-washing cloth. Adam carried the water out for her, and then went to look in his saddlebag at the week-end's homework: nobody ever looked at it on a Friday evening. Nan saw his good example, and went to find her own books; so Mary was left with the eggs laid out all round her, dirty on her left, clean and drying on the right.

'I'm only going to look at it,' said Adam. 'I always look at it early: then it does itself during the day, and I write it down at night.'

'That's what makes you forget things,' said Mary. 'But I've written an egg for you. It's a brown one: they're the best, but they're not so good for selling.'

'People would rather buy white ones,' said Nan.

'Or blue ones,' said Mary. 'Why don't we keep starlings?'

'They don't lay enough eggs: only about six in a whole year. But hens are mad: they lay them all the time.'

'And bigger ones too,' said Mary. 'Anyway, we don't know so very easily where the starlings are; but the hens are in the henhouse.'

Breakfast was ready when the eggs were washed. Adam put his books right away. 'Two simultaneous quadratics,' he said. 'On difference of factorials, one rule of three, and the rest plain donkeywork about recurring decimals. And an essay on astronomy.'

'Stars,' said Nan.

Mary tried to remember what stars were like; but during the day she could not imagine the sky black, and blossomed with the pinched points of the stars.

When breakfast was over, and the freshly written eggs eaten, Nan entered the number of washed ones in the book, packed the boxes, and wrote the labels. Mary and Mother washed up. Adam thought about astronomy in the garden, and pulled up dandelions, and looked at the house-plan of the garden beds.

Mary came to him when the housework was done, and told him they had to explore under the Yat and find a way into Fairyland.

'I'd rather paint,' said Adam. 'And what shall we find?'

'We might just see the way in,' said Mary. 'There must be one. I expect when we get near we shall hear the dogs inside. We might have to dig a hole to help them. They might have grown bigger, or something.'

'They might,' said Adam. 'We'll go that way if you like, but I'm going to paint, and I don't mind if you can't find any way in anywhere.'

Mary gave him a knowing look: it was one she had borrowed from school, and she used it when she felt cleverer than somebody else. She went to get the grass rope with its red ribbon and drying tassels of balsam grass.

'Does it have to be green?' she said. 'It's turned into hay, you know.'

'The unicorn will eat it,' said Adam. Mary wound the rope round her waist and held it in with her belt.

During breakfast Charley had taken the tractor and gone up to mend the wall between the intakes and the roughest pasture.

'He's where he was last week,' said Nan. 'He only does it on Saturdays, I think.'

'I wonder if Peter heard the tractor,' said Adam. 'It's a straight line between the farm and where Charley is and the Yat.'

'Ask Charley if he's heard Peter,' said Nan.

Charley was chipping a stone with the walling hammer so that it would fit an odd corner.

'You mind how you jump off them walls,' he said. 'If you go straight up ower you'll coome to t' corner, where yon old wall butts again t' edge o' t' fell. Now you mind t' pit in t' corner. You've nobbut to fall off t' wall—and nobody will never find you.'

'We saw it once,' said Adam. 'Very deep.'

'Aye,' said Charley. 'Thou drop a stone in it, and tha'll see it's none so very soft either.'

'We aren't going to fall down,' said Adam. 'But it would be very easy. It's exactly where you'd cross the wall if you were going to the Yat: if you go anywhere else you have to climb two walls, unless you go right round the end of that one across there.' He meant the wall that Charley was taking down: it stretched a hundred yards across the pasture, and no farther.

'Yon's a sackless bit o' wall,' said Charley. 'But happen it's grand to take a bit off from to make this 'un higher. T' sheep is more jumpy than they were: Mester Owland gets his grass too good for 'em.'

They left Charley and went on up the pasture.

'He only said the sheep were too jumpy because he doesn't like spreading lime and stuff,' said Nan.

'Nobody does,' said Adam. 'Mary, don't get over the wall.'

'I want to see the pit,' said Mary, who thought she knew what it was.

'You only want to see the top of it,' said Adam.

'It goes right down into the bottom of the world,' said Nan. 'It's all rocks and water inside.'

Mary said no more about it until she saw the square hole in the fell, with the old rusty wire fence round it to keep the sheep away, and then she said 'Yes' to herself because she felt sure this was a way down to another world, not only to the bottom of this one.

Adam and Mary and Nan sat on the wall and looked.

'I've seen it before,' said Adam. 'And I shouldn't like to fall down it.'

'Does it really go down a long way?' said Mary, making certain.

'I told you,' said Nan. 'It goes down ever so far.'

'Listen,' said Adam. He found a stone, and cast it down the shaft in the way he had before. Again the stone fell in silence. Then it struck rock, slammed itself away again, and went down in a noisy skirring spin into more rocks.

'Not into water this time,' said Adam.

'Plain rock is worse,' said Nan.

'Doesn't sound very plain to me,' said Adam. 'Rather knobbly and decorated with spikes, I should say.'

'Did you hear them buzzing?' said Mary.

'Only one stone,' said Adam. 'It twists as it goes.'

'They were angry,' said Mary. 'Flying away from the stone. You shouldn't tease them, you know.'

'It wasn't fairies,' said Nan. 'The same thing happened last time we dropped a stone down.'

'Then you've made them angry twice,' said Mary. 'Tell them you're sorry.'

'We aren't,' said Adam. But Mary thought they should be forgiven: she called down: 'They are sorry really, and they won't do it again.'

Adam helped Mary down from the wall, and led the way round the pit. Mary stayed behind for a moment, now that she had found a place where fairies lived and could be heard, though they were out of sight and no one at all could get there. She left them something to remember her by, in case they had the unicorn down there and so that they could make it tame and ready for her. She undid her

belt, took off the grass rope, coiled it tightly, and threw it over the brink, ribbon and all; and it vanished. She thought she heard it slither on rocks; then there was silence below but for the water agitating among the rocks.

Nan came back for her and herded her along to Adam. They walked over the lumpy ground to the foot of the Yat.

'It's like a castle wall,' said Adam. 'You expect to see archers at windows.'

'Doorway to the fairies,' said Mary. She listened carefully here, but there was no noise from anywhere, except the common blowing of the wind.

'Well, aren't you going to look for it?' said Adam.

'No,' said Mary. 'No need.' She knew now where the entrance was; and one day there would be a barking and a crying from it, and out would climb a pack of yellow dogs. It might take seven years; but they would come.

'We'll go on,' said Adam. They crossed the ridge, and came out on the south side of the pass, with Vendale below them: a hundred fields between the steep sides where the wood grew under the fells.

Peter stood in front of the inn. He saw them and waved. 'Wait for him,' said Mary.

'He may not want to come all the way up,' said Nan.

'Don't tell me so many things,' said Mary. 'He can walk down with us, and that will be all right.'

Peter and Hewlin were not long coming up beside the Dig and on to the fell.

'I've been waiting for you,' said Peter. 'Have you got something up here?'

'No,' said Adam. 'Where were the foxes we saw?'

Mary jumped up to see the place. Peter took them a little way down the hill to where the grass was short and bright on a smooth bank.

'They were laiking here,' he said. 'But you won't see owt.'

Nan waited for Mary to start talking about where the foxes lived. As soon as she started Nan was going to show her the small place where the water of the Dig came out of the hill.

Mary said: 'Where did they go away to? Oh, off with the fairies, perhaps.'

'Yes,' said Nan, knowing nothing of Mary's decision that the mineshaft was a way into fairyland. 'They probably went in where Dyson got drowned, at the top of the Dig.'

'Show me,' said Mary anxiously, hoping that the place would look quite wrong, so that she wouldn't have sent the grass rope down to the wrong people.

Nan led the way to the top of the water. The hillside went up in a narrow overbrowing cliff, where Dyson had dug in his attempt to reach Fairyland. The water came out of a narrow cleft, as high as a man at first, with the roof sloping down towards the back. Out of the hole the water ran, tumbled straight down a step of rock, cut its way through a soft bank, and then started its wild staircase to the valley below.

'How big is a unicorn?' said Mary, looking at the small place the water came from.

'Quite big,' said Nan. 'But small enough to get through there,' she added at once.

'Oh,' said Mary. She advanced beside the water. It came out of a little tunnel: now it was running smoothly, and stones lay in it. Mary put her face against the water and looked into the hill.

'What can you see?' said Adam.

'Something,' said Mary. 'I've got my pigtails wet.'

'And you've dropped your grass rope in the Dig,' said Peter. He picked it out of the water and gave it to her.

'Isn't there a unicorn?' said Mary, taking the rope.

'No,' said Peter. 'Only a hair band.'

'I wonder why,' said Mary, because she could think of no reason why the fairies should send back the rope without a unicorn on it; unless it was the wrong kind of rope.

'Or perhaps they want me to come again,' she said. 'And they'll send something out.'

'Why?' said Nan: her idea seemed to have worked: Mary appeared to think this was the unattainable gate to Fairyland.

'I know why,' said Mary. But she said nothing about what she had seen inside the hill: Nan was right; there was a white light within, and green growing things: Fairyland.

CHAPTER SIXTEEN

THE GATEWAY

'Did you see any foxes?' said Adam.

'No,' said Mary. What she had seen she would not talk about. 'There's all that painting you haven't done.'

'I've been waiting for you to finish scuffling about,' said Adam.

Mary was still scuffling about wringing water from her hair and from the grass rope.

'You should have tied it on more tightly,' said Nan. But Mary only smiled at that: Nan did not know where the grass rope had been: down into Fairyland by one door and out again through another secretly; nobody knew but Mary. She thought Adam might know something about it, because he said the unicorn would eat the green rope: and in the middle of the rope there was a fresh thin place where the strands were nibbled or chafed away. Mary coiled the rope up into a small bundle, and went down the hill with the others. She knew what she must do as soon as the time came.

'Come by, Hewlin honey: they're making pictures today,' said Peter. Hewlin came down the hill with his wriggling walk.

'I suppose,' said Adam, 'that his collar is what I ought to paint: a silver one, not golden.'

'That's the mark,' said Peter. 'But it's not been brightened, so don't paint it black: use white paint instead.'

The light of day had almost gone when Nan closed the gate after the egg-van, and it went slowly down the bank with a wave from the driver.

Nan and Mary stood on the gate, and watched the red lamp disappearing in the grey light under the Bank. The van went round the first twist: now there was only the flat road between black walls.

'Let's go and meet Adam,' said Nan.

They climbed the gate into the road. Mary stood on the milk-churn stand to find out whether she could see over the pass into Vendale and the opening into Fairyland.

'What does dancing to fiddles sound like?' she asked.

'Can't explain,' said Nan, when she had thought about it. 'Come on, or he'll go the other way, and we'll never find him.'

They walked along in the dusk. The sky hung high overhead in colours of new roses; and to the west lavender and marigold; to the east the green of sage, and under the cloud that rolled behind the sunset the edge of darkness came on: silver lined like a well edged with daisies.

'What colour are we?' said Mary. 'All grey and white like that dead woodlouse I found under the rug on the landing?'

'Dream colour,' said Nan.

Adam walked across the intakes whistling.

'I'll call him,' said Nan.

'Don't,' said Mary. 'You'll frighten the foxes.'

'Not so very much,' said Nan, and she shouted to Adam. He came to the road and walked back to Lew Farm with them that way: over the gate, and across the scar, starting up the rabbits and making them sprint. Mary skipped and scampered all round the other two: soon the time would be here when she had something to do; and nobody else could do any of it, because no one else knew about it: except perhaps the foxes.

'I've finished the unicorn's horn,' said Adam. 'And a blue sky: when I saw the sunset I thought it was a pity; but a blue sky is good all the year round, and a red and green one might look wrong in winter.'

Mother was waiting at home to see that everybody went promptly to bed properly washed.

'I'm tired of all this bedness,' said Mary. 'And if you wash me it makes me sleepy.'

'A very good idea,' said Mother. 'You're tired and excited, and you won't want to get up in the morning. But I think I'll put you quickly through the bath, because there isn't a clean inch on you.'

'I'm quite capable of being clean,' said Mary, giving Mother a knowing look.

'And I'm quite capable of getting you clean,' said Mother, who knew Mary was using words without their meanings. 'Up you come.'

Mary did not want to go to bed: she particularly wanted to stay awake; a thing very hard to do once your head is put on the pillow and kissed, and you have let your warm feet find the cool corners of the sheets. Mary left her head on the pillow when Mother had kissed her. To keep herself awake she thought of what she had to do. That reminded her of an important thing. She sent Nan to get her some biscuits.

'Put them in a bag,' she said.

'What for?' said Nan. 'Won't a plate do?'

'A bag,' said Mary. 'Then I shan't drop them.'

'Crumbs, you mean,' said Nan. 'Would you like some water as well?'

'Not in a bag,' said Mary. 'Not any water: I shan't be thirsty.'

There were eight biscuits in the bag. She put it beside her bed. Eight would be enough; perhaps a lump of sugar would have been a good thing too; but biscuits would do. She looked at the bag. Now it was only a whiteness against the dark walls. Dog biscuits would have been best of all, she thought. Then she was asleep.

She woke up to a sound unusual for the middle of the night. Somebody was running a bath. There was light from outside, where the moon sent down its soft bright candlebeams; and light from the landing. Mary saw Adam walk across, and heard him close the bathroom door and turn on the cold tap.

She got out of bed. Now was the time: she had slept exactly long enough: over the dark and into the day made by the moon in the middle of the night.

The rest of the house was quiet. Mary found her socks and put them on by moonlight the right way out. She was about to put on the dress she had worn during the day, and then she thought her nighty would be better because it was longer and more like a dancing dress. She put it on again, and waisted it with the sash of her school tunic: it had softly fringed ends. On top she put a cardigan, because it had long sleeves. A pair of black dancing pumps went on to her feet, and she was ready. No; there was one more thing: she took out both her hair ribbons and shook her hair loose. In the mirror she thought her moonlit self was beautiful.

She took the bag of biscuits and left the moonlight for the bright landing. Adam splashed in the bath. Nan was singing to herself in bed: just as Mary passed her door she went to sleep. Mother and Daddy were talking in the kitchen. Mary thought she might come back before they went to bed: they would hear her return and come to meet her, not knowing what it was.

Out of the door; pick up the grass rope; and there ahead was the extra day of moonlight: and the dancing under the hill: but she could hear no music yet. She left the farm garth and climbed the gable of Thoradale among the sleepy sheep. The moonlight was warm; later on there would be processions in it, and a whole family of dogs, and a prize strong unicorn.

Mary hurried up the intake, through a sheep gate in the wall; and she was in Vendale.

A quarter of an hour later she was looking down on the Dig and listening; and thinking she could hear the treble violins fairy-dancing. She went down close to the water, and it flooded away in its falling all music but its own.

Mary climbed up beside the water, and came into the earth darkness close to the side of the hill. The water was below her now, carrying its sound with it: all but the strong gush that first came out of the hill. In the darkness Mary put her head close to the water, holding her loose hair and the bag of biscuits in one hand, and the tightly rolled grass rope in the other.

There was light inside the hill; and something moved: but there was no music.

'When I get inside,' said Mary. And to go in she must crawl in the water. A minute later the hillside was empty: Mary was on the stones in the tunnel.

At Lew Farm Adam coaxed the last rim of soap scum from the bath, dried behind his ears again, because they still felt damp, and left the bathroom.

Mrs Owland came upstairs as he came out with the lamp in his hand.

'Good night,' she said.

'Good night,' said Adam.

Downstairs Mr Owland locked the back door. Adam walked to his room slowly, so that the lamp flame stayed low and did not lick a dark staining tongue up the glass.

Mrs Owland unhooked the hanging lamp on the landing, turned it right down, and went to see whether Nan was asleep. She went into Mary's room to pull another blanket over her. She came out at once and hung the lamp up. She thought Mary had gone into her bed. When she looked there she found no Mary.

'Has Mary pinched your bed?' she asked Adam.

'No,' said Adam.

'In the bathroom, I expect,' said Mrs Owland. 'She must have nipped across when I looked at Nan. Probably playing with the candle, making black patterns under the bath.'

'I wonder where she is,' said Mrs Owland again, when she had looked in the bathroom. She and Daddy looked in the rest of the house: there was no Mary.

'Do you think she's gone out?' said Mother.

Nan was awake now. 'I didn't hear her.'

'What's she wearing?' said Daddy.

Mother looked to see what was left. 'She seems to be wearing everything but her dress and her shoes: all the rest has gone, including her nighty. Her hair ribbons are here too.'

'She's taken her dancing pumps,' said Nan. 'And her bag of biscuits.'

'Biscuits?' said Mother.

'She sent me to get some when I was coming to bed,' said Nan. 'She wanted them in a bag; but she wasn't thirsty.'

'Wasn't thirsty?' said Mother.

'She didn't want a drink of water as well,' said Nan.

'Then where's she gone?' said Daddy.

'The Dig,' said Nan. 'We went there this morning, and she said she might have to go back.'

'Where else did you go?' said Daddy.

'The inn,' said Nan.

'The Yat,' said Adam. 'Talking about fairies all the time. We went past the pit.'

'Good God,' said Daddy. 'The mineshaft. Adam, come with me. Mother, stay here. If a cloud comes over the moon the child will be completely lost.'

'What about waking Charley?' said Mother.

'No time,' said Daddy. He ran downstairs to light a lantern. Adam ran after him pulling on a sweater.

'I'll go and tell Charley,' said Nan. 'He can come with me to the Dig.'

'No,' said Mother. But Nan had gone in her pyjamas as she was, running down to the tractor shed and getting her bicycle, and riding down in the moonlight with bare toes on the cold pedals.

Charley was locking his front door when she got there. 'What is it?' he said. 'Hasta found another o' them foxes?'

'Mary's gone out alone,' said Nan.

'T' li'l bairn all alone?' said Charley.

'Come with me to the Dig,' said Nan. 'Daddy's gone to the mineshaft.'

'By Gow,' said Charley. 'She'll be drowned or else break herself from together.'

'No,' said Nan.

'Nay,' said Charley. 'That's t' worst. Or is she carried off by fairies?'

'Yes,' said Nan. 'And that's seven years.'

'Don't take on,' said Charley. 'Theer's nowt in that. We'll be for off: Ah've me lantern by.'

Daddy and Adam ran up the intakes, over the wall, and into the pasture. The fell lay like a lawn in front of them, ridged with the walls, and bounded by the stark cliff of the Yat, and only the sky beyond.

'Where the walls join,' said Adam, showing the way.

They ran on, and the pale lantern light jogged with them. The sheep lifted their black faces and chewed. A moon-hunting owl mewed down the dale; the moonlight lay like still water.

The mouth of the pit was black. The sides were touched by the moonlight.

'I'll shout,' said Mr Owland. 'A devil of a lot of use that will be. Tie the rope to something.' He took a breath and shouted: 'MARY.'

There was a moment's silence whilst the shout flung it-

self down the dale and over the pass. 'Doesn't get us anywhere,' he said, and shouted again: 'M A R Y.'

Before the echoes had gone from the fells there came an
answer, far away below his feet, from the depths of the pit.

'Be quiet,' said Mary. 'You've frightened them away,
and I'd only got one of them.'

CHAPTER SEVENTEEN

IN FAIRYLAND

When Mary vanished from the hillside and went into the place where the water of the Dig came out, she had several things to look after. The grass rope was the most important: it would not matter if it got wet, but it must not be lost: the reason for coming here was the unicorn, and a grass rope is what you must bring. Another anxiety was the bag of biscuits. They would be useful for two things: one was to catch the hounds with; and perhaps the unicorn would have to be tempted: and Mary herself must have something to eat, because it is not safe to eat anything given to you when you are with the fairies. Other things to be kept in mind were her hair, because she had brought no comb, or anything to dry it with if it got wet; and the long skirt of the nighty, because that would be uncomfortably wet, and there would be no one to iron it dry the way Mother had done it the other evening.

With all these things in mind one after another, Mary knelt in the water. She found her knees were not in the water, but upon stone, and her hands, feeling carefully in the dark water, found more stone ahead. The stone was not dry, but it was better than seven or eight inches of fast water.

Mary was in a little tunnel. There was darkness all round her: no way of telling what was beside and above and below. Ahead there was light, not a bright light, but a soft gentle illumination.

Mary crawled. A hand and a knee, a hand and a knee. The roof of the tunnel hit her head; it hit her shoulder; it hit each knob on her backbone. The tunnel walls came in and scraped her wrists and her knees and her ankles. She stopped crawling and put the bag of biscuits inside her cardigan, and tucked the nighty up again. She listened for music, but there was only the water immediately underneath her. Even if there was no music there was still the light in front, showing steadily: if that was still there then the fairies were still there, though they might be resting from the dance, not knowing who was coming through the passage.

'Don't be frightened,' she said. 'I'm bringing the grass rope.'

She knew there was somebody there: she saw them move among the green plants.

Then she was out of the tunnel, though still in the dark. She was beside the water now, a little cold, but not so wet as she had expected. She shook out her hair and hoped it was tidy, rubbed her knees dry on her cardigan sleeves, and opened the bag of biscuits, ready to get one out if she met a hound. The grass rope she kept coiled, and hoped the unicorn would not mind that it was wet.

Now she was ready. But there was still no music: only the sound of the little gill in a cavernous valley. Mary walked on through willow herb and catching bramble and fingering fern, and came into the light.

She was in a small glade, and all round was complete darkness, with tall things just showing in grey on every side.

A forest, thought Mary. A forest under the fell. And she listened again for music; but there was none.

Besides the sound of the water there was another noise. Something moved a stone and sneezed. A grasshopper chirred among the ferns; Mary knew that was music.

She walked into the middle of the lighted glade. She found she had scarcely a shadow. In the middle of the glade the ground was hard rock, and in the middle of the patch of rock sat the thing that had sneezed.

It looked at her with bright eyes, and sneezed again, because it had a feather on its nose.

'You poor little dear,' said Mary, and offered it a biscuit. It looked at the biscuit and turned its head away. Mary put the biscuit back in the bag.

'I thought all dogs liked biscuits,' she said. 'Shall I stroke you?'

There was no answer. Mary put down the grass rope, and stroked with her left hand, scratching the animal's forehead and tickling behind its ears.

'You shan't have to go back with the others,' said Mary. 'I'll tie you up and take you to Hewlin, not all alone, of course, my dear, but with the others, and the unicorn, so I can't use my grass rope on you. But come with me and we'll look. Are you frightened of the trees?'

It was afraid to walk, she thought. She left it, and looked in the glade for something to leash it with.

Willow herb—no, nor bramble, nor fern. She looked on

the ground: there might be something there. There was, and she found it. In a gravelly place on the rock, where the water sometimes ran, she discovered a number of things that would do.

'There's some wire here,' she said. 'I think it's barbed wire without any sharpnesses. It won't hurt you.'

There were a good many fragments. She gathered them all up into her lap and brought them back to the middle of the glade.

'Don't pull very hard,' she said. 'This is an old wire, and it might break where I've twisted it together if you pull too hard.'

She made the pieces into a long rope or chain, bending the soft metal round into hooks and linking the pieces together. Then she slipped an end round the neck of the bright-eyed animal beside her, and there it was on collar and chain.

'I must fasten you to something,' she said. 'I must go into the forest and find the others, and the unicorn. If you would just bark and call for them they would run back and find you.'

A sneeze was the answer. Mary took the feather away from its nose. Then she went round the glade in the light, looking for something to fasten the chain to. There was nothing growing that would do: the brambles were too thin, and the trees looked too big. Mary could see how high they were without turning her face up to the sky.

There was something in a place between two rocks: a long white stick with no bark.

'This will do,' she said. 'I can push the thin end into the ground, and the other end's still fixed to part of the tree, with holes in. I expect they're birds' nests, but there aren't any there now. But I can fasten your chain through the holes.'

That was easy: the chain came through one of the holes, and Mary hooked it back into itself. Finding a place to drive the stick in was not so easy: there was no soft ground. At last she found a crack in the rock and pushed the point of the stick in; and that would do, she thought.

'Now I'm going into the forest,' she said. 'But I won't eat anything of theirs, and I'll soon come back.'

She turned away, and as she walked beside the water ready to go into the unknown darkness under the trees, there was a voice she knew shouting her own name very loud.

'MARY.'

She turned round. The chained animal was standing up, and the chain was stretched taut.

'Come back,' said Mary. 'You promised, you know.'

There came a second shout: 'M A R Y,' and the animal ran away, and with it went chain and stick, all into the cavy darkness towards the tunnel: and at once they had gone.

'Be quiet,' said Mary loudly. 'You've frightened them away, and I'd only got one of them.'

'What are you doing down there? How did you get there?' called Daddy.

'I'm not down,' said Mary. 'I came in by the doorway. Go away. I'm fetching dogs and a unicorn.'

'Come back this moment,' said Daddy. 'Where is the doorway?'

'In the Dig,' said Mary. 'How did *you* get in?'

She heard Daddy talking to somebody. 'Stay where you are,' he called.

Mary sat down beside the water. Daddy might have a lantern with him, and that would be best for walking in the forest. She waited. If she was quiet perhaps the hound would come back.

Mary and her captive were not the only ones disturbed by Mr Owland's shout. The sound had gone up to the Yat, and echoed down to the Unicorn Inn. Hewlin leapt off Peter's bed so thumpily that Peter woke up in time to hear the second shout. Mrs Dyson heard them both, and she came to Peter's window to listen again.

'There's something up,' said Peter.

'There is,' said Mrs Dyson. 'Get a lantern, Peter. There's somebody up against the Dig with a light. We'll be up and see what's on.'

The lantern at the Dig belonged to Charley. He had run on in front of Nan, though he could hardly see by moonlight. On the hill beside the water he almost stumbled against some invisible animal. He heard it run away, and after it something rattled and dragged; but it was gone before he brought the lantern round and steady.

'Nowt to do wi' it,' he said, and ran on.

He came to where the water ran from the hill. He put his head down into the mouth of the tunnel.

'Are ya theer, Mary?' he called.

'Charley,' said Mary, 'have you brought a lantern?'

'By Gow,' said Charley to himself. 'That I have,' he said. 'Wheer art tha?'

'Fairyland,' said Mary. 'But it's dark.'

'Ah don't doubt it is,' said Charley. 'And is it wet?'

'Not up here,' said Mary. 'It's a sort of sunshine, but it's dark under the trees.'

'Coome and get t' lantern, then,' said Charley.

'I will,' said Mary. 'You haven't caught one of the hounds, have you?'

'Nay,' said Charley. 'Nowt here.'

Nan came clambering beside the water, out of the moonlight and up to the lantern.

'She's inside,' said Charley. 'And cooming out to get t' lantern. Fairyland, she says.'

'I told her it would be,' said Nan.

Mr Owland and Adam came over the hill, short-breathed and swinging their lantern.

'Hush,' said Charley. 'T' lass is on t' road out.'

'There'll have to be some explanations,' said Daddy. 'And there was no need for you to come out, Nan.'

They were joined by somebody else.

'What's all this for?' said Mrs Dyson.

'Heaven knows,' said Mr Owland. 'Mary's in there. . . .'

'Then show her a light,' said Mrs Dyson. 'Don't stand there gaping.'

There was a noise in the tunnel: the stones were shifting under Mary's weight. Then came her head, with her hair in a great tangle. She put out her hand.

'I don't think Daddy could get in here,' she said. 'Just give me the lantern.'

'What the dickens are you talking about?' said Daddy. 'Come out this moment.'

Charley lifted her out. Three lanterns shone on her.

'You didn't need to all come,' she said. 'Nan, it was right: there's Fairyland in there, and I caught one hound, but Daddy frightened it off into the forest. I want to go back and get it.'

'Fairyland?' said Daddy. 'No such thing! You've been into a very dangerous and silly place. Do you *know* where you were?'

'Yes,' said Mary, not sure any more, and quite distressed at being scolded.

'You don't,' said Daddy. 'You've been in the bottom of the mineshaft.'

'Not a forest?' said Mary.

'No,' said Daddy.

'But there was a dog,' said Mary. She felt cold and wet and small and disbelieved; and she had left the grass rope in the tunnel and forgotten it.

'Come thy ways, honey,' said Mrs Dyson, picking her up. 'Why, the bairn's soaked and frozen: only in her nightie, too.'

'My dress wasn't long enough,' said Mary. 'For dancing.'

'And didn't you get any dancing?' said Mrs Dyson. 'Now you come down and stop the night with me, and we'll see about Fairyland in the morning.'

'Nay, Hewlin,' said Peter. 'Come by.'

'Women,' said Daddy.

'You were ower sharp,' said Charley.

'I was,' said Mr Owland. 'We'd better go home. Come on, Nan.'

But Nan had gone with Mrs Dyson.

CHAPTER EIGHTEEN

THE UNICORN CAPTURED

'Well, you moppets,' said Mother. 'Perhaps you'd like some clothes.'

'It wouldn't be so very nice to go to church in these,' said Mary. She was wearing a pair of Peter's grown-out-of pyjamas; Nan wore her own. They were having late breakfast in the kitchen of the inn. Daddy and Mother had driven across early with Adam and Charley. Charley had gone up the Dig, Adam went into the stable, and Daddy with him to see what the inn sign would be like.

Nan and Mary dressed; Peter fed Hewlin on bacon rind and crusts; Mrs Dyson and Mother talked, half about rug-making, and half about the night before.

When Nan and Mary were dressed everybody came into the kitchen, except Charley, who was busy on the hillside.

'Now,' said Mother. 'I want to hear the whole story.'

'It isn't Mary's fault,' said Nan.

'I don't think it's anybody's fault,' said Daddy. 'We just want to know how it came about that Mary was discovered in the middle of the night at the bottom of a deep pit.'

'*I* know about it,' said Mary.

'Everybody's done something,' said Peter. 'But it was Adam started it.'

'Go on,' said Mr Owland.

'Me?' said Adam. 'Well, I came to get the treasure if I could. You know, what Gertrude Owland lost when she was eloped with.'

'The first Dyson,' said Mrs Dyson. 'Him that got drowned.'

'Yes,' said Adam. 'That was all. I'd heard about the legend of the hounds and the unicorn, and what happened at the Dig, so I came to see what the common-sense explanation was.'

'I think I know what it was,' said Mr Owland. 'But go on somebody: what happened next?'

'Some unicorns,' said Nan.

'None of them much good,' said Adam. 'I hadn't any clues, you see, so I polished the paint off the signboard, and looked for useful marks.'

'And words,' said Mary.

'Come and have your hair brushed,' said Mother. 'I brought the brush.'

'There was a gold collar,' said Peter, 'and there was the silver collar on our Hewlin. But nowt else.'

'Until we discovered the trumpet,' said Mary. 'And the name on the other hound.'

'Mary did that,' said Adam. 'But I was already beginning to have an idea about it, though I couldn't make out what it was. Anyway . . .'

'Aye,' said Peter. 'Anyroad, I . . .'

'You did,' said Mrs Dyson. 'The night the cow got on the roof, I call it. I never heard such a din. There was some what for about it, I can tell you.'

'There was that,' said Peter, looking sideways at the hairbrush in Mrs Owland's hand.

'After that I knew what Dyson had done,' said Adam. 'But it still didn't make sense, because the hounds would have come running back to Lew Farm as soon as they lost themselves under the Yat.'

'Unless they got themselves right bangled,' said Peter.

'Only two stayed out,' said Adam. 'Hewlin and Belanter.'

Hewlin looked at everybody in turn, hoping that they were talking about bacon rind.

'The rest went to Fairyland,' said Mary.

'Hmn,' said Adam, disbelievingly.

'Mary's right,' said Daddy. 'If Fairyland is where she says it is.'

'What?' said Adam. 'How?'

'The hounds and the unicorn went somewhere,' said Mr Owland. 'All but the lame one, Belanter, and the deaf one, Hewlin. So, where did they go? Now, if you walk straight up from Lew Farm to the Yat, you have to go round the mineshaft. If you don't go round you go down. Have you noticed how the walls come together at the shaft?'

'Yes,' said Adam. 'You come to the shaft very easily, because it's where there's only one wall between the intakes and the fell.'

'The fell wall and the one that Charley's taking down both together make a sort of lead-in to the shaft,' said Mr Owland. 'That's where the dogs and the unicorn went down. What could be easier?'

'Complete with the silver collars,' said Adam. 'Well I never. Over the wall, and snap, down they went.'

'Quite,' said Mr Owland.

'Why didn't Dyson get a rope and go down after them?' said Nan.

'There's a simple explanation,' said Daddy.

'I don't know what it would be,' said Nan.

'The shaft was full of water,' said Daddy. 'Perhaps not quite full, but with enough in it to make it impossible to get the collars out. The dogs would drown, and then sink to the bottom, you see. And Dyson did try to get them out.'

'Why let them get into water at all?' said Adam. 'He would know they would be difficult to get out.'

'He didn't know he would want to get them out,' said Mr Owland. 'He didn't know until after he'd drowned them that they were carrying treasure.'

'That's why Sir Thingummy Owland laughed himself to death,' said Nan. 'How did Dyson try to get them out, Daddy?'

'You know,' said Daddy.

'The Dig,' said Nan.

'Exactly. He knew where the shaft was, so he tunnelled into this side of the hill to find the bottom of it.'

'And he did,' said Nan. 'But all the water ran out and drowned him in it.'

'Took him to Wassand Church,' said Peter. 'He shouldn't laike with Owland girls. There's only bats and what for and getting up in the night if you do.'

'They're bad lots, aren't they?' said Mr Owland, pulling Mary's newly-made pigtails.

'But what about Fairyland?' said Nan.

'Mary's right,' said Daddy. 'She went into the very place where the hounds and the unicorn went. But it wasn't Fairyland: only the bottom of the pit.'

'I thought there were trees,' said Mary. 'It must be Fairyland if the dogs were there.'

'Call it what you like,' said Daddy. 'But you won't get there again—not even you, Adam. Charley's gone up to put iron bars across the tunnel.'

'A good thing too,' said Mrs Dyson. 'Or we'd have our Peter drowned for sure.'

'But,' said Mary. 'What about the dog?'

'Part of a dream,' said Daddy. 'You were nearly sleep-walking, you know.'

'Well,' said Mrs Dyson. 'This isn't getting the house-work done.' She had very little housework to do on Sunday, but she thought she might prevent Mary from quarrelling over the dog and whether it was real or imaginary; because no one would ever see it to settle the question.

'I tied it up with little bits of wire that must have fallen down from the fence at the top,' said Mary. 'But it ran away.'

'It's been lost six or seven hundred years already,' said Daddy. 'Another few hundred won't matter. Come on: Mrs Dyson wants to wash up.'

They all went out but Mrs Dyson and Mother, who stayed behind to wash up and talk.

'There was a dog,' said Mary as she went.

'Don't be silly, dear,' said Mother.

Daddy opened the front door of the inn, and met Charley.

'Put yon Hewlin back inside,' said Charley. 'And coome out and say nowt.'

'Why,' said Mary, looking out past Daddy. 'That's the hound.'

Charley was standing in the forecourt holding a stick. From the stick hung a chain, and on the chain was a fox cub, sitting miserable but inquisitive in the sunshine.

'Good Lord,' said Daddy. 'You did catch something after all, young woman.'

'Yes,' said Mary. 'It's mine. I just caught it. It was sitting down and it sneezed.'

'It were fast in a sheep yat in t' intake,' said Charley. 'Ah'd nobbut to pick it out. What will Ah do wi' it, Mester Owland?'

'It's Mary's,' said Mr Owland. 'She'd better have it. But it mustn't come in the house. And it had better stay on a chain.'

'It'll want a new one,' said Charley.

'Yes, it will,' said Mary. 'I only made that one. But it didn't break.'

'T' cub got its neck fast,' said Charley. 'Happen Mister Owland shot its mum. What it wants is a good suck o' milk, and a bit o' mothering. And for all that it'll be off next spring, wild again.'

'It'll always stay with me,' said Mary. She took the

chain from Charley, and knelt beside the fox to stroke it again.

'Our Hewlin would go for that,' said Peter. But Peter himself went forward to make friends.

'Ah've fixed up them bars,' said Charley. 'There won't be nowt gets in there now.'

'Good,' said Mr Owland.

Adam spoke to Nan. 'I think it's bad,' he said. 'But it's the best thing really. All the same, I should have liked to look inside for the treasure.'

"Specially the unicorn's horn,' said Nan.

'Never mind,' said Adam. 'I'd better get on with the signboard.'

Peter had found something interesting on the fox.

'Adam,' he said. 'Look at this here.'

'Don't fuss round,' said Mary.

'Aye,' said Charley. 'Don't fright it: if you do they smell like all and owt.'

'It's not the fox,' said Adam. 'It's the chain—the wire Mary used for its collar. Look at it.'

'Mary's right again,' said Daddy. 'It may not be the hound; it may not be Fairyland; but this is all made of the lost silver collars.'

'Let's have them off,' said Adam.

'Quick,' said Mary. She pulled off her hair ribbons and made another collar for the fox. Adam unhooked the silver chain, and looped the whole length of it over his arm.

'I shall call you Belanter,' said Mary.

'There's nine of them,' said Adam. 'What an odd piece of wood you've fixed it to, Mary.'

'Looks like the top of an animal's skull, but made of wood,' said Daddy.

'It's bone,' said Adam. 'Two eyes and one horn. What animal has the horn in the middle of its forehead?'

'Unicorn,' said Nan.

'Don't be silly,' said Adam, going red with astonishment at being told he was holding in his hand the skull of an imaginary animal.

'It is and all,' said Peter. 'Our Mary's as miraculous as owt.'

'It can't be,' said Adam.

'Look at it,' said Mr Owland. 'There's only one horn, and there it is in the middle, isn't it?'

'Yes,' said Adam. 'But there aren't such things.'

'I can see it,' said Mary. 'So it must be there.'

'It is there,' said Adam. 'A genuine unicorn's skull. I shall believe in Fairyland next.'

Peter went in to tell his mother about it. She came out with Mrs Owland, both full of curiosity. But she had no time to look at dead skulls; she picked up the fox cub, said: 'Whilst you stand gimmering there this little one will starve,' and took it and Mary indoors. 'I'm used to pups,' she said. 'Fox and all—they all need the bottle.'

'She'll soon have it as cobby as owt,' said Peter.

Adam unlinked the nine silver collars. Hewlin came out, and his collar was compared with the others.

'His is blacker, and more worn down like,' said Peter.

'More used,' said Adam. 'But silver's silver. Unicorns are—well, unicorns.'

'I don't think it's quite so strange as it looks,' said Mr Owland. 'It's not very hard to grow unicorns—in the right country, that is, not England.'

'Go on,' said Adam. 'There must be an explanation. What is it?'

'Don't tell us,' said Nan. 'I don't want to hear.'

'Don't listen,' said Daddy. Nan blocked her ears whilst Daddy explained to Adam.

Mary came out when Daddy had finished.

'It's drinking milk and milk and milk,' she said. 'Mrs Dyson says they're cleverer than dogs.'

'I did tell you not to find one,' said Mother. 'But I suppose you couldn't help it.'

'I did think it was a dog,' said Mary. 'But I'm glad it isn't.' She ran inside again to watch the cub at the bottle.

Peter came out with the silver polish. 'We'll brighten them,' he said. So Mr and Mrs Owland, Charley, Nan, Peter and Adam, sat on the bench and polished silver collars; and Hewlin gazed at the unicorn's horn, and hoped somebody would offer it to him.

By and by Mary and Mrs Dyson came out with the sleeping cub, and helped to polish the last two collars.

'One for each of us, and one for each animal,' said Mary. 'And all because I believe in fairies.'